A CHRISTMAS AMISH COURTSHIP

JENNIFER SPREDEMANN

A CHRISTMAS AMISH COURTSHIP

(AMISH COURTSHIP SERIES) BOOK 3

JENNIFER SPREDEMANN

Published in Indiana by *Blessed Publishing*.

www.jenniferspredemann.com

All Scripture quotations are taken from the *King James Version* of the *Holy Bible.*

Cover design by *Blessed Designs* ©

Paperback ISBN: 978-1-940492-95-7

10 9 8 7 6 5 4 3 2 1

KEEP UP WITH THE LATEST JENNIFER SPREDEMANN NEWS

Get a FREE Amish story as my thank you gift when you sign up for my newsletter at: www.jenniferspredemann.com

BOOKS BY JENNIFER SPREDEMANN

AMISH BY ACCIDENT TRILOGY

Amish by Accident

*Englisch on Purpose (*Prequel to *Amish by Accident)*

*Christmas in Paradise (*Sequel to *Amish by Accident*) (co-authored with Brandi Gabriel)

AMISH SECRETS SERIES

An Unforgivable Secret - Amish Secrets 1

A Secret Encounter - Amish Secrets 2

A Secret of the Heart - Amish Secrets 3

An Undeniable Secret - Amish Secrets 4

A Secret Sacrifice - Amish Secrets 5 (co-authored with Brandi Gabriel)

A Secret of the Soul - Amish Secrets 6

A Secret Christmas – Amish Secrets 2.5 (co-authored with Brandi Gabriel)

KING FAMILY SAGA (AMISH ROMANCES)

An Amish Reward (Isaac)

An Amish Deception (Jacob)

An Amish Honor (Joseph)

An Amish Blessing (Ruth)

An Amish Betrayal (David)

AMISH COUNTRY BRIDES

The Trespasser (Amish Country Brides) 1

The Heartbreaker (Amish Country Brides) 2

The Charmer (Amish Country Brides) 3

The Drifter (Amish Country Brides) 4

The Giver (Amish Country Brides Christmas) 5

The Teacher (Amish Country Brides) 6

The Widower (Amish Country Brides) 7

The Keeper (Amish Country Brides) 8

The Pretender (Amish Country Brides) 9

The Arranger (Amish Country Brides) 10

The Healer (Amish Country Brides) 11

The Newcomer (Amish Country Brides) The Prequel 12

UNLIKELY AMISH CHRISTMAS

Unlikely Santa

Unlikely Sweethearts

Unlikely Singing

Unlikely Season

AMISH COURTSHIP SERIES

A Forbidden Amish Courtship

A Widower's Amish Courtship

A Christmas Amish Courtship

FAIRY TALES

The Princess and the Prayer Kapp (Cindy's Story & Rosabelle's Story)

OTHER

Learning to Love – Saul's Story (Sequel to Chloe's Revelation)

Her Amish Identity

An Unexpected Christmas Gift

COMING 2023 (Lord Willing)

Unlikely Sacrifice

BOOKS BY J.E.B. SPREDEMANN

AMISH GIRLS SERIES

Joanna's Struggle

Danika's Journey

Chloe's Revelation

Susanna's Surprise

Annie's Decision

Abigail's Triumph

Brooke's Quest

Leah's Legacy

A Christmas of Mercy – Amish Girls Holiday

Unofficial Glossary of Pennsylvania Dutch Words

Ach – Oh

Ach du liebe – Expression similar to "Oh, my goodness!" or "Oh, dear!"

Allrecht - All right/alright

Bann – Shunning/excommunication

Boppli/Bopplin – Baby/Babies

Bruder/Brieder – Brother/Brothers

Daed/Dat – Dad

Denki – Thanks

Der Herr – The Lord

Der Welt – The world

Dietsch – Pennsylvania German

Dochder(n) – Daughter(s)

Dumm – Dumb

Dummkopp – Dummy

Englischer – A non-Amish person

Ferhoodled – Crazy, scatterbrained, mind is elsewhere

Fraa – Wife/Missus

G'may – Members of an Amish fellowship

Gott – God

Gross sohn – Grandson

Gut – Good

Haus – House

Herr – Mister/Lord

Hochmut – Proud

Jah – Yes

Kapp – Amish head covering for women

Kinner – Children

Kumm – Come

Lieb – Love

Libeling — Little One

Maed/Maedel – Girls/Girl

Mamm – Mom

Nee – No

Ordnung – Rules followed by the Amish church (varies according to district)

Schatzi – Sweetheart (my treasure)

Schweschder(n) – Sister(s)

Sohn – Son

The family way – Pregnant

Vatter – Father

Verboten – Forbidden

Wunderbaar – Wonderful

AUTHOR'S NOTE

The Amish/Mennonite people and their communities differ one from another. There are, in fact, no two Amish communities exactly alike. It is this premise on which this book is written. I have taken cautious steps to assure the authenticity of Amish practices and customs. Old Order Amish and New Order Amish may be portrayed in this work of fiction and may differ from some communities. Although the book may be set in a certain locality, the practices featured in the book may not necessarily reflect that particular district's beliefs or culture. This book is purely fictional and built around a fictional community, even though you may see similarities to real-life people, practices, and occurrences.

We, as *Englischers*, can learn a lot from the Plain People and their simple way of life. Their hard work, close-knit family life, and concern for others are to be applauded. As the Lord wills, may this special culture continue to be respected and remain so for many centuries to come, and may the light of God's salvation reach their hearts.

PROLOGUE

No matter how hard Anne Eicher tried, she couldn't push the thought away. How could it be that her younger *schweschder* was happily married and she was still at home—alone. Thanks to Johnny Hershberger.

She stared at the late November snowflakes floating down just outside the window and shoved a tear away. Why was she still crying over him? He obviously hadn't felt the same affection toward her, even though they'd courted for so long. Why had he strung her along all this time only to leave?

Jah, she'd been brave in front of her family because she didn't want Charlotte to feel bad that Andy Stoltzfus, her former beau, had roped his cousin Johnny into leaving the community with him. But if she were honest with herself, she *did* blame Andy. Sure, he'd left, nursing a broken heart over losing Charlotte to Glen Kauffman. But to take Johnny along after she'd already waited five years for him to propose was just cruel.

She remembered the day in vivid detail.

Andy Stoltzfus had marched into the house as though he lived there. She'd identified several emotions as they'd flitted across his face. Anger. Sadness. Regret. Disillusionment.

"I'm leaving the community," he'd admitted to Anne and her *dat*.

Dat hadn't tried to talk him out of it but let him speak his mind.

"Charlotte has chosen Glen Kauffman over me. I can't bear to see them together—to see them wed. I just thought you should know." Then he'd pivoted toward Anne. "I'm sorry, Anne, but Johnny's leaving too."

Her mouth had hung open and it took her a few moments before she could speak, before his words could register. "Johnny's leaving?"

What about the last five years of her life that she'd devoted to him, waited for him, until he was ready to begin their happily ever after? What of that? If he'd had in mind to desert her, why had he strung her along all this time?

It all seemed so unjust.

She'd been beyond ready to settle down, marry, begin a family of her own. But now, she couldn't see that happening.

And just the thought of showing up at a singing without knowing Johnny would take her home caused the knife in her heart to wedge in deeper.

Nee, her days of attending singings were over. A closed chapter in the book of her life. Besides, if *Der Herr* wanted her to marry, surely He'd bring someone along.

Ach, who was she kidding? The chances of her finding someone to marry now were slim at best. She'd held out hope for Johnny while all the other *maed* her age found their matches and were now living their blissfully happy married lives.

Gott, if there is someone out there for me, please make me aware of him.

CHAPTER 1

Andy Stoltzfus had been pondering the situation for some time now.

He wasn't sure when the exact moment was that he'd decided to go through with his harebrained idea.

It could have been the moment he'd left the Eichers' home after witnessing his would-be fiancée in the arms of another man. He still scowled as he relived the hurtful moment when he'd caught Charlotte and Glen in a lip lock under the covered bridge and overheard Glen's proposal of marriage.

He wasn't sure why he'd been surprised, though. Because, if he'd been honest with himself, he'd known somewhere deep inside the recesses of his heart that Charlotte had been falling for Glen Kauffman. He'd tried with all his might to convince himself otherwise, but denying the truth had only resulted in more heartache.

He batted the unsavory thoughts from his mind, staring at the pen and blank paper on his desk. He needed to focus.

He knew that *this* was his chance when his cousin Johnny declared he wasn't going to return to the Amish. Which meant he wouldn't be returning to Anne Eicher. Which meant she was free to court someone else for the first time in over five years.

But Andy knew he couldn't just show up on her doorstep and ask to court her. Neither could he take her home from a singing. Rumor had it that she hadn't returned to the youth events since Johnny had abandoned her. Besides, he had a pretty *gut* feeling she'd turn him down flat if he asked.

The first reason being that he'd recently courted her younger *schweschder*. The second reason being he'd whisked Johnny away from the community. In her eyes, anyway. He'd read it in their depths when he'd declared their departure. Did she *still* blame him for Johnny's absence? He hoped that wasn't the case and that someday he'd be able to explain the whole truth of the matter.

He sighed, removed his spectacles, and rubbed his eyes. This was more trying than he'd imagined. A simple letter admitting his feelings for Anne was all he needed to write. She could respond how she wanted. Or she could ignore his letter altogether.

Or.

Or...what if he wrote a different kind of letter? One where his identity remained anonymous. The idea burgeoned in his chest.

A secret admirer.

He frowned. Was that too weird? Too creepy, as his younger *schweschder* would say?

No mind. The idea had already taken form and he was nearly helpless to stop it.

He set pen to paper and the words seemed to flow effortlessly. His eyes scanned the words he'd penned.

Gott, I pray I am doing the right thing. Please let this work.

ANNE REACHED her gloved hand into the mailbox at the end of their driveway and grasped the bundle of mail. No doubt another stack of Christmas cards. She wouldn't sift through it now, lest the brisk wind snatch an envelope from her hand and send her scurrying across the snow-covered ground to fetch it.

She tugged her wool coat tighter and hastened to the house. She would read through their Christmas cards as she sat by the cozy fireplace with a hot beverage in hand. Thankfully, she'd finished all her morning chores and could stand to take a break until the *kinner* arrived home from school wanting snacks.

Since *Mamm* had passed away several years ago, it seemed that Anne had taken her mother's role upon herself. As the eldest *dochder*, she'd felt it was her duty and privilege. And now that Charlotte was married off, she'd taken her role even more seriously. After all, Jane and the boys needed tending to.

She quickly shed her coat, scarf, and gloves and went about fixing some apple cider.

When the *kinner* returned from school, she'd prepare a fresh batch of popcorn—one of their family's favorite snacks and something *Dat* hadn't minded since they'd purchased the kernels in bulk at auction. Anne appreciated the ease of popping the kernels and how quickly the snack came together. It had been a staple in the homes of most Amish families she knew, for that reason. One never knew when company would drop by and the need for a quick snack would arise.

As Anne melted into her favorite chair, she set her cider on the side table and began sorting through the mail. Seven festive Christmas cards, two letters, and... she stopped when an envelope with her name caught her eye. Turning it over, she searched for the sender's name, but only found a return address. A post office box in Ohio.

Ach, likely junk mail. She opened the fireplace to toss it inside, but curiosity niggled at a place in her mind. She shut the stove's door and sighed. It wouldn't hurt to peek inside. After all, the neat writing did appear to be penned by a human hand and not a typewriter.

Dear Anne,

You're probably curious about why you are receiving a letter with no return name. The fact is, I wish to remain anonymous. For now.

We've been acquainted with each other for quite some time now.

I have watched you over the years and I've come to deeply admire you and your commitment to the wellbeing of others. I've never known anybody like you.

I have a proposition I'd like to share with you. This is going to sound strange, and if the idea does not interest you, then I won't write to you anymore.

Here is my idea: You and I will write no less than one letter a month to each other over the course of a year. In each letter, we reveal something about ourselves. Then, next November—a year from now, if you are agreeable, we will meet in person and marry before Christmas of next year.

If this doesn't intrigue you at all, or if it's too crazy a notion to consider, please let me know in your return letter.

Sincerely,
A Secret Admirer

P. S. In case you're wondering, I am Amish.

ANNE SCANNED THE LETTER AGAIN, her mouth hanging open.

Ach, she had so many questions. Who was this unidentified Amish man who had apparently been watching her for years? She considered all the young men in their district and couldn't imagine who the letter might be from.

And he wanted to *marry* her? She could never marry a stranger. Not even one who apparently adored her. Which was a little creepy. And, if she admitted, sweet.

Why did this man feel the need to send her letters and not engage face to face? Why didn't he want her to know who he was? It felt a little unfair that he seemed to know her, but *his* identity had to remain a mystery.

Well, never mind. She'd set the letter aside and study it again later after she had some time to pray about the matter.

She opened up each Christmas card and made a note of each one so she could return the favor.

But as she read through the remainder of the mail, the anonymous letter called to her.

Married by Christmas next year?

Ach, the very idea seemed preposterous, given the five years she and Johnny had courted with nary a solid proposal from him.

Married by Christmas next year.

The happy thought settled somewhere between her ribs. Visions of holding a *boppli* in her arms in less than two years played on the silver screen inside her head and she couldn't squelch a smile.

It was a *ferhoodled* notion, to be sure.

She didn't know who this man was, but for the first time in years, she felt...*cherished*.

CHAPTER 2

After careful prayer and consideration, Anne made a decision. As crazy as the notion sounded, she would write back to this mystery man.

But she determined to keep her expectations to a minimum. Weren't expectations said to destroy relationships? Not that they had an actual relationship.

She'd tread circumspectly and keep her innermost thoughts to herself. This stranger didn't need to know about her fanciful daydreams.

Dear Secret Admirer,

I admit that I am curious.

However, I'm a little alarmed that

you think I would marry a stranger. With that said, I am intrigued by the proposition. I don't mind writing to you if you are lonely and in need of a friend.

Marriage, on the other hand, isn't something I'm hoping for at this time. I had hoped to marry someone, but that person has disappeared from my life.

How did you say you know me? Since you are Amish, and your letter is postmarked Ohio, I'm guessing you live in another community.

Only a Friend,
Anne Eicher

SHE EXAMINED the words one more time. She'd alluded to not being interested in marriage, which wasn't entirely true. But that was why she'd added the phrase "at this time". It was better to get to know one another as friends anyhow.

Perhaps that would keep his expectations low as well?

All she knew was that she hoped she wasn't getting in over her head. What harm could a few letters to a lonely soul bring?

ANDY WANTED to jump for joy the moment he spotted the letter in his post office box. She'd written back!

But before he could get too excited, he'd better read the letter. No telling what it might read like. For all he knew, it could just be a polite response indicating she wasn't interested and demand he stop writing to her.

As soon as he reached the buggy and shimmied inside, he slipped his pocketknife through the sealed envelope flap.

A smile bloomed on his face that he couldn't contain. She had agreed to write! He squeezed his eyes closed and sent a brief prayer of thanksgiving heavenward. *Denki, Gott!*

ANNE NEEDED to stop her daydreaming. The family would be joining them for supper tonight, so she needed to focus on the task at hand. Not imagining what the anonymous letter writer would say in his next letter.

Charlotte burst through the door from the *dawdi haus*, all smiles. It seemed she'd been bright and cheerful every day since she and Glen had married, and she'd moved into the dwelling attached to their main home. Love seemed to sparkle in her eyes.

"I came to help. Just came from the mailbox." Charlotte handed Anne an envelope. "This looks like a letter for you."

Already? It had only been a few days since she'd responded. Anne tugged her bottom lip between her teeth.

"Who's it from?" Had her *schweschder* always been this nosy? Yes, she had.

Anne warred with whether to share her secrets with her *schweschder*. *Ach*, what would it hurt?

She shrugged. "I don't know."

"What do you mean?"

Anne threw the apron on over her head, tied it, then went to fetch the first letter.

Charlotte's smiled widened as she opened the letter and read it. "A secret admirer?" Her *schweschder* gasped and her hand flew to her heart. "*Ach*, this is so sweet. And terribly romantic."

Anne laughed at her sister's reaction. "You don't think it's weird?"

"I mean, *jah*, it's different for sure." She pinned her sister with a look. "Who do you think it is?"

"I have no idea. I've been trying to think of all the folks we know in Ohio."

Charlotte tapped her lips. "Do you think it's someone who came to Sammy's or mine and Glen's wedding?"

Anne shrugged. "That's kind of what I was thinking. I just can't imagine who it could be."

"He says he's been watching you for years. That's...interesting." Charlotte's nose scrunched up. "It almost makes it seem like someone in our district."

"I don't recognize the handwriting at all. Do you?"

Charlotte examined the letter. "What if he's not writing in his usual way?"

"Like a disguise? That would be difficult to maintain, don't you think?"

"I suppose."

Charlotte bounced on her toes. "Well, are you going to open that one?" She pointed to the unopened letter in Anne's hands.

"In private, yes."

"Okay. I'll leave and come back." And just like that, her *schweschder* had disappeared into the *dawdi haus.*

Anne supposed she could stand to take a short

break. She retreated to her bedroom and sank into the chair at her desk.

Dear Anne,

Thank you for writing back to me.

If friendship is what you have to offer, then I accept. Although, if I'm being honest, I do have hopes that our friendship will deepen into something more. But please, do not think I will pressure you into anything.

I know what it's like to think you have something secure and then have it suddenly slip through your hands. I'm sorry you have experienced a lost love as well. I understand your hesitance where marriage is concerned.

As far as being Amish, I am living in Ohio. To add too many details, I fear, will give my identity away, so I'll just leave it at that.

Since we're sharing a little about ourselves in each letter, here is something I can tell you about me. I enjoy making things with my hands. Whether it be wood, leather, metal, I like to take something ordinary or broken and turn it into something beautiful.

Kind of like what God does when we allow Him to work in our lives. That is something I'm learning right now.

Enough about me, though. What do you enjoy?

Sincerely,
Your New Friend

WAS IT ANNE'S IMAGINATION, or did her heart do a little flip at his mention of *Gott*? One thing she never liked about Johnny Hershberger was that he didn't seem to have a care for the things of God. It had been something that bothered her, as her folks had always been adamant about reading the Bible and encouraged all their *kinner* to do likewise.

Perhaps she should consider this letter writer more seriously. In addition to his mention of *Der Herr*, he did seem to have *gut* spelling and grammar skills, and his words had been penned with care. Didn't that say something about a man?

She did admit, like Charlotte had claimed, that the idea was romantic in a way. And she knew, from dating Johnny all those years and hearing stories of others' courtships, that romantic men were few and far between.

With a renewed sense of intrigue, she pulled out her stationery and favorite writing pen.

CHAPTER 3

Besides Anne Eicher's letter, there was one other piece of mail Andy had been waiting on.

He'd sent a note to Bishop Omar letting him know that he would be returning to the community soon. He also asked after Fannie Byler, the current schoolteacher who was expecting a *boppli*, and whether they'd found a replacement teacher or not.

He had previously filled in for a teacher who'd been in a similar predicament and found that teaching the scholars suited him. He enjoyed seeing the *kinner* learn and grow and discover a world of possibilities only limited by their own imagination.

The letter had finally arrived today, and it seemed as though *Gott* had been answering many of his prayers as of late. First, Anne. Now, this.

Since he'd been actively attending one of their sister churches, Bishop Omar had only needed to confirm the fact with the sister church's bishop. The bishop had been cooperative, and Bishop Omar welcomed Andy back into the community with open arms.

He'd even made a concession for Andy regarding his vacant property. He'd received permission to purchase a small travel trailer to live in while he worked on building his home during his spare hours. It helped immensely that school ended at two thirty. There would still be a couple hours of daylight when he returned home to the camper each evening to work on his future home.

And if all went as he hoped, by this time next year he'd be moving into a completed house carrying his bride over the threshold. And maybe it was presumptuous, but he'd hinted as much to Bishop Omar.

Ach, Gott. Let it be so.

It seemed as though *Gott* had timed everything just right. His letter to the bishop. Fannie Byler's leave of absence. His move back to his folks' community.

He wished he had someone to share his excitement with, but he quickly realized Johnny wasn't that person. So far, he'd been skeptical about the things Andy had shared, so he decided it would just be better to offer his thanksgiving to *Gott*.

And if he moved back, he was quite certain Anne wouldn't suspect the letters were coming from him. She thought she was writing to a man in Ohio, which had been true at the onset. He saw no need to correct her assumptions that he still lived there.

With that being the case, it removed a lot of pressure from his shoulders. He'd simply be Teacher Andy who'd had his heart broken by her *schweschder* and no one would be the wiser.

It was a fool-proof plan, wasn't it?

"HOW WAS SCHOOL TODAY?" Anne continued kneading the dough for rolls as her two youngest siblings clambered through the door and sunk down at the table.

"Okay, I guess." Her youngest *bruder,* Zane, harrumphed.

"*Wunderbaar*!" Jane said at the same time.

Anne chuckled. "Want to tell me what happened?"

Zane shook his head.

"Teacher wants us to be Mary and Joseph in the Christmas program!" Jane volunteered. "He's been a pickle because he'd rather have another *maedel* be Mary."

"I would not!" Zane protested. "She thinks I like someone."

"It's true. He does." Jane continued. "And Teacher wants you to make our costumes."

"And bake cookies," Zane said, finally showing some enthusiasm. "May I have a snack? I'm starved."

"That's 'cause he gave his lunch to Becky Zook."

Zane nudged Jane's shoulder. "You're not supposed to tell."

"He likes her." Jane added.

"I do not." Zane frowned. "She didn't have nothing to eat."

"Anything." Jane corrected.

Anne nodded to the apples and bananas on the table. "Help yourself."

She thought about the Zook family. Becky's *mamm* had been in and out of the hospital, but the doctors didn't know what was wrong with her. Becky was their youngest *maedel* and the only one still in school.

"Maybe we can pack extra for your lunch tomorrow. It's kind of you to share, but I don't want you going hungry either."

"Teacher said we were going to make a blessing box. Do you know what that is?" Jane chomped on an apple.

"*Jah*, I know what a blessing box is. I'll have to stop

by the schoolhouse and drop some things off, or I could just send some jars with you. We still have a lot of tomatoes in the basement from the summer harvest. I'll check and see what else we can give."

Zane made a face. "I don't think they like tomatoes."

"He means *he* doesn't like them." Jane snickered.

"Just because *you* don't like them doesn't mean that others don't. They're *gut* to use in recipes. Even *you* like them in spaghetti." Anne reminded.

"I reckon." Zane conceded.

"Alright, you two. Time to get your chores done. Your *bruder* and *schweschder* and their families are going to be joining us for supper tonight."

"I get to hold the *boppli*!" Jane's voice carried through the hall as the *kinner* went to change into their choring clothes.

Between Glen's three-year-old *dochder*, Grace, and Sammy and Roberta's little *bu* Walt, there would be plenty of excitement at supper tonight.

Anne pondered the *kinner*. They were growing up quickly, but Jane was ill-equipped and too immature to run a household. Sometimes Anne wondered if the girl had a domestic bone in her body.

Either way, even if her letter writer did want to marry next year and if she agreed to marry him, there would be no way she could leave home. Since *Mamm* passed, most of the household duties had fallen on her shoulders. What would *Dat* and the *kinner* do without someone to wash their clothes, make them meals, and sew new outfits?

Was a year enough time to train Jane in these things? *Ach*, she would need to step up her *schweschder's* training. Besides, Charlotte was still living next door in the *dawdi haus* with her young family and could offer assistance if necessary.

"Jane, come help with supper preparations as soon as you've gathered the eggs." Anne called to her *schweschder* and didn't miss her groan as she scampered out the door in a rush.

Like as not, Jane needed to learn.

Had *she* been that difficult when *Mamm* taught her? She didn't think so.

She'd been sixteen when *Mamm* passed, and at the time, she didn't think she'd ever be able to fill *Mamm's* shoes. Yet, she had. Of course, having Charlotte here to help out meant they'd shared the responsibility.

Now, she was twenty-three and contemplating running a household of her own. *Twenty-three?* Had it already been seven years since *Mamm* had gone to Heaven? Her heart squeezed tight, stealing her breath.

"*Ach*, *Mamm*. I miss you so much," Anne whispered into the now-quiet kitchen, allowing her tears to fall.

WHILE WAITING for the rolls to bake, Anne had been pondering her letters and what they could eventually lead to.

What if they agreed to meet at some point and she found him utterly unattractive? Not that she was vain and needed a man that would only suit for a catalog model. But attraction, although not the main ingredient in a relationship, did carry importance. You wouldn't want to sit across the table or wake up every day next to someone you had a hard time looking at. *Ach*, perhaps she *was* vain.

But didn't true love overcome even that? Or transform the person you've come to love into someone attractive. *Gut* looks weren't everything.

If only *Mamm* were still around to ask about these kinds of things. Surely, she'd have some advice about the letters.

Their guests poured into the house all at once and Sammy's *fraa,* Roberta, dismissed herself to the bedroom to change the *boppli*. Anne's *schweschder* Jane, and Glen's *dochder* Grace, accompanied her, no doubt seeking an opportunity to hold the *boppli* after his diaper change.

"What's that frown for?" Her *bruder* Sammy

sidled up to her, examining her countenance. *Ach*, Sammy. Always the intuitive one.

"*Ach*, nothing." Anne shook her head, dismissing her previous thoughts.

"She got a letter," Charlotte blurted out, then lifted a smirk. "From a secret admirer." She sang the words.

"Really?" Sammy grinned, seeming more relaxed now.

Anne shot their sister an evil eye. "Charlotte!"

"I think it's sweet. Not everyone gets secret letters." Charlotte placed her hands over her heart, and all but swooned.

"Hey! Have I been doing this all wrong?" Glen grumped at his *fraa's* reaction.

"Apparently, we both have." Sammy chuckled. "Who would have thought *maed* would get so excited over a silly letter?"

"It's not silly, it's romantic, *dummkopp*." Charlotte nudged their older brother with her shoulder. "Something I'm sure your wife would appreciate every once in a while."

"I give her flowers," Sammy protested.

"Flowers are boring. Everyone does that." Charlotte turned to Glen. "No offense, *Schatzi*."

"What do you consider romantic, besides a letter?" Glen asked this time.

Was he taking notes? That in itself was a romantic gesture, Anne mused.

Charlotte grinned. "To me, romance is doing something or giving something that speaks to the soul. For example, you know that I love covered bridges. And because of that, you planned to take me to see all the covered bridges in Indiana."

Sammy snorted. "He may have ulterior motives."

Glen pushed Sammy's shoulder and shook his head, but Anne didn't miss the shushing motion Glen gave Sammy behind Charlotte's back. Everyone knew what sweethearts did inside covered bridges.

A slow smile spread across Charlotte's lips, as though she were recalling a special moment in one of those bridges.

Anne remembered a few of the moments she and Johnny had shared at the bridge. She was sure their initials were still carved on one of the beams inside. He'd carved *J+A Forever* inside a big heart. Forever had been short-lived.

"Still. It shows that he listens to me, and he cares about the things I care about. It's sweet." Charlotte leaned over and pecked a kiss on Glen's cheek.

Anne felt a small tug on her apron, then she glanced down. Little Grace held out a wrapped gift.

Anne smiled and caught her *schweschder's* eye. "What's this?"

Charlotte shrugged. "She couldn't wait until Christmas." She and Glen shared an adorable look.

Anne accepted the gift from little Grace's hand. "*Denki, liebling.*"

She opened the package wrapped in Snoopy cartoons and pulled out a small hot pad. "*Ach*, this is *wunderbaar*!" She made a big deal for the sake of the little one. "Did you get this for me?"

Grace nodded. "I made it. Me and *mamm*." She smiled at Charlotte.

"Well, I love it." She pulled Grace close and kissed her cheek. "You did a *wunderbaar* job! *Denki* so much. I think we'll use it right now. Do you want to put it on the table?"

Grace nodded.

Anne's heart warmed. What would it be like to have her own little girl to teach how to sew and bake? *Gott, if it's Your will...*

Within ten minutes, their entire clan had arrived. *Dat* and Clive had thankfully removed their smelly boots and left them in the mudroom before washing up for supper. As soon as *Dat* took his seat, everyone else scurried to theirs, then *Dat* bowed his head in prayer.

CHAPTER 4

Since Anne had an errand to run, she'd decided to drive by the schoolhouse to see if she could catch the teacher before she left for the day. Perhaps she was still in the schoolhouse correcting papers or preparing for tomorrow's lesson.

Sure enough, a buggy still waited in the small shed and a horse whinnied from the inside stall. She'd heard a noise on the other side of the building, so she opted to see if the teacher might be outside.

When Anne rounded the corner, she'd been unprepared for what she saw.

A man, at least eight inches taller than her five-foot-five inches, hefted a maul and swung it down hard, cracking through the stump of wood.

Since his back was turned, she stood quietly appraising his stature. His shirt fit his broad shoulders well but strained as he worked. His strong back tapered to a trim waist. Arm muscles, exposed by his rolled-up sleeves, flexed and bulged as he swung the heavy maul. And she knew how heavy those things were, barely being able to swing one herself.

She found herself wondering who this well-put-together man was, and her cheeks heated as she realized she'd been appreciating, or rather gawking at, his raw masculinity. *Ach*, what if he was a *dat* to one of the scholars? The thought shamed her.

Was this the replacement teacher for Fannie? She hadn't expected a man. She cleared her throat, and he spun around. Her eyes widened.

Ach, she hadn't been expecting Andy Stoltzfus. "Andy? *You're* the new teacher?"

"Just a substitute for now." His voice was a low rumble that tickled her insides. This was Andy Stoltzfus, for crying out loud. Her *schweschder's* former beau.

Her *schweschder's* former *single* beau. She banished the foolish thought as soon as it surfaced.

"I hadn't realized you'd come back to the community."

"Probably because it's officially my first day back, although I've been coming to the schoolhouse." A gentle smile curved his lips.

Had he always been this attractive? Probably. She'd been so enamored with his cousin Johnny

Hershberger that she'd forgotten all other handsome men existed.

The short span of silence ended with his question. "How is your family?"

She knew he was probably asking after Charlotte, who'd broken the poor man's heart. "They're *gut*. And yours?"

"I haven't really been home yet." He studied her and frowned. "Johnny didn't come back with me, if you're wondering."

She wasn't.

She gave a slow nod. As far as she and Johnny went, they were done. That chapter in her life had closed, never to be reopened again.

"Listen, Anne." He reached out and touched her forearm, the heat of his fingers seeping through her dress sleeve. "I'm really sorry about what happened."

She held up a hand to stop his words, breaking his hold. "It's okay. I'm over it. Thinking back on it now, we probably should have broken up a long time ago."

"I wish I could help you, somehow. I feel bad." He frowned. "If you must know, I didn't talk Johnny into going with me. He'd been set on leaving for quite a while. I guess he just saw that as his chance."

She sighed, not wanting to think about Johnny anymore. She'd already lent him too many of her thoughts, as it was. She needed to change the subject.

Back to why she'd come in the first place. "The *kinner* said you needed some garments made for the Christmas play?"

"*Ach, jah.*" He nodded in recognition. "That's why you've come."

"Well, I was in the area and spotted the buggy, so I thought now was as good a time as any."

He nodded and gestured to the schoolhouse.

The stack of firewood all but forgotten, she followed him as he rounded the front, ascended the steps, and opened the door wide.

HE TRAILED Anne into the schoolhouse and studied her as she took in her surroundings. It felt *gut* to have her here in his space. Like they were sharing something personal.

Andy couldn't believe his *gut* fortune.

Had the girl he'd been dreaming about literally just shown up out of the blue? He tossed up a prayer, thankful *Gott* had nudged him to chop more firewood. Otherwise, he would have headed home already.

Since Bishop Omar had approved his purchasing a small trailer to keep on his property while he worked on his house, he'd decided to stay there as much as possible. He hadn't felt like returning home to live with his folks after he'd experienced what it was like to live on his own. Of course, he and Johnny shared an apartment, but he felt more independent than he'd ever been, and something about it made him feel more like his own man instead of his parents' child.

It seemed like he'd grown up years within the past few months. It had given him clarity on many things. Perhaps he should thank Charlotte. Their breakup had been difficult, but it turned out to be a blessing in disguise.

Although he'd moved into the small trailer on his property in Indiana, he would keep his post office box in Ohio open as long as he and Anne were corresponding. Since both locations were near the border, it was only about an hour drive by car.

"I like this." Anne pointed to the writing assignment he'd given the *kinner*.

Her voice drew him from his musings. How could he forget she was there? In the flesh. In his classroom? He recovered. "I wanted to open their eyes to the value of family."

"I think it's important. Not everyone comes from a *gut* place. Sometimes, we don't realize how blessed we really are."

"*Jah*, the bishop spoke to me about some issues our community has had. I won't go into detail. But he thinks that if the *kinner* have an outlet to express their thoughts, we can catch issues early and deal with them head-on."

She gave an understanding nod. "You're talking about abuse."

"*Jah*. It's sad to think about the depravity of man and the sin that so easily besets us."

"That's why it's important to follow after *Gott's* ways, I think. We get into less trouble when our focus is on Him."

"You're a wise woman, Anne Eicher."

A smile bloomed on her face at his words and appreciation reflected in the depths of her gaze. Then she shook her head. "Not so wise. I've had good guidance from my folks. They always encouraged us to seek *Gott* on all matters. The only wisdom I might have comes from *Der Herr*."

With each word she spoke, Andy was reminded why he'd fallen so hard for her. "I see you're modest too."

She shook her head, and her cheeks flushed a beautiful pink hue, reminding him of an autumn sunset.

He pulled the script for the Christmas play out of his desk. "We'll be going through the story of Jesus' birth, and I've chosen Zane and Jane to play Joseph and Mary since they're good with all the lines. Zane also has a poem he'll be reciting, and Jane insisted you'll be bringing her favorite cookies."

"The girl does love her chocolate. Can't say I blame her." A shy smile lifted the corners of her lips. "Do you have a favorite cookie?"

"That's easy. Gingersnaps."

"Truly?"

"*Jah*, why? I know that's not a typical favorite cookie but—"

"Gingersnaps are my favorite too."

"*Ach*, for real? I think you're the first person I've met who shares my obsession."

Her face brightened. "I don't know if I'd call it an obsession." Then she frowned. "Sadly, I haven't been able to perfect the recipe."

"I could give you my *mamm's* recipe."

"*Denki*. But I'm afraid that even with a recipe, they still don't turn out right. You see, when *Mamm* was still with us, she used to make them for me all the time." She swallowed. "I have her recipe. Hers were *wunderbaar*, but mine just aren't the same."

"I see." He wondered if maybe her emotions were influencing her perception. Why did it seem like food and experiences were always better when you were with a loved one? He'd realized this fact when he'd gone to get an ice cream cone at one of the places he and Charlotte had previously visited. He ended up not even finishing his cone and tossing it into the trash because it had been so disappointing.

An idea formed in his head. "Maybe it has something to do with the process. I could arrange for you to come over one day to make them with *Mamm*, if you'd like."

She fiddled with her bottom lip. Had she seen through his thinly veiled attempt to spend more time with her?

She shrugged. "I guess I could."

"*Wunderbaar*!" *Ach*, he needed to curb his enthusiasm. "I'll talk to *Mamm* and get word to you. Is there a day that's best?"

"Any day the *kinner* are in school would be best for me."

Right. He had to force himself not to frown. If it was during school, he wouldn't be able to join them. There went that brilliant idea.

"*Ach*, okay. I'll let you know." He swallowed. He'd just have to show up at the Eichers' to deliver the time and day *Mamm* was available. A visit wouldn't last as long as it would have been if he joined the women baking cookies, but at least it was something.

An idea sparked. "Just be sure to swing by the schoolhouse when you're done so I can do a taste test."

"I see." She laughed. "You really are obsessed, aren't you?"

"You have no idea." He chuckled, his double meaning going unnoticed.

ANNE NEEDED to finish her letter before the mail carrier arrived. Her conversation with Andy Stoltzfus had given her an idea. She looked down at her letter and grinned at the question.

What is your favorite kind of cookie?

CHAPTER 5

Andy stared down at the letter and grimaced.

Oh dear. I guess I walked right into this one, didn't I?

He laughed at the craziness of it all.

One thing he knew for sure. He couldn't respond to Anne's question with *gingersnaps*. For sure and certain that would give him away. He supposed he could ignore it altogether, but that would be rude and might cast suspicion.

Ach, he'd have to shelf it for now until he could come up with a *gut* honest answer. He read the letter over again, loving that he held a piece of her in his hands.

Hello again, friend.

I don't know about you, but I've

been busy here. With Thanksgiving over and Christmas coming soon, I seem to have a full plate.

Dad continues to manage the feedstore (I'm not sure if you already knew that Dad had a feedstore or not!), most of the outdoor chores have fallen to my nineteen-year-old brother Clive (I don't think he minds), my two youngest siblings (Jane and Zane) are still in school. Earlier this year, my sister Charlotte married and moved into the dawdi haus with her husband Glen and his little girl, Grace. Sammy lives down the road a spell with his wife and baby boy.

That leaves me to run the household—cooking, baking, cleaning, sewing, laundry. Not that I'm complaining. Since my mother passed on several years ago, I've pretty much taken over her role. I'm not quite sure what they will do once I'm gone. Jane is simply too young and immature to take over these duties on her own. These are things that I tend to worry over.

Anyhow, our family seems to be growing quickly. And if I had to guess, might be expanding again soon.

Enough about all that. I wish I could see some of your woodwork. That sounds like an interesting and creative thing to do.

I enjoy baking. I sew some too, but not as much as my sister, Charlotte. But I have a project to work on for the kinner's Christmas program at school, so I'll be sewing more soon. Maybe I'll see about making a couple of Christmas gifts. My brother Sammy's son seems to grow each time I see him, so I'm sure my sister-in-law would appreciate some clothes for him.

There I go, rambling again. Sorry.

Just one more thing before I close this letter. What is your favorite kind of cookie?

Your friend,

Anne

ANNE WAS happy to have her *schweschder* just next door to occasionally help with chores. It was like she'd moved, but she was still there. Anne grasped another clothespin to hang the dress she'd washed on the clothesline.

She turned to her *schweschder*. "Charlotte, did you know Andy Stoltzfus is back and he's teaching the *kinner* at the school?"

Her sister's mouth opened, then she shook her head. "I had no idea. Zane or Jane didn't say anything?"

"Not that I can remember." Of course, her mind had been elsewhere since Johnny Hershberger ghosted her.

Charlotte pinned a pair of Glen's trousers on the line. She had been happy to make new Amish clothes for her husband and his *dochder* after they'd left the *Englich*. "Well, *gut*. Hopefully, that means that he's moved on and forgotten about me."

Anne snorted. "Not likely. He did ask after the family. I assumed he meant you."

"*Ach.*" Charlotte frowned. "Wait. When did you see him?"

"I stopped by the school the other day. He was outside chopping wood." *Jah*, she'd recalled that image more times than she would ever admit. She couldn't help biting her lip at the thought. "He did seem older, somehow."

"Interesting."

"*Jah*, I thought so." She wouldn't mention Andy's offer to make cookies with his *mamm*. No need for Charlotte to get any romantic ideas.

It seems she'd had enough of those herself lately.

"Any more letters?" Charlotte's grin grew. Speaking of romance...

"I haven't checked the mail today, but I'm not expecting one yet. I just sent one off yesterday."

"I have a feeling you're enjoying this." Charlotte always seemed to have a smile on her face when they discussed the letters.

"I am, actually. The letters are going back and forth a lot more often than I expected. I doubt it will ever lead to much. But we seem to have some things in common."

"Like what?"

"I can't really put a finger on it. But he mentioned *Gott*. Johnny never talked about *Der Herr*." Anne shrugged. "Does that sound strange to you?"

"*Nee*. Not really."

"I guess it just made my heart happy to know that he thinks about *Gott*. Know what I mean?"

"*Jah*. So, he makes your heart happy?" Charlotte's eyes twinkled.

"Don't make this any more than it is." Anne sighed. It was better not to get anyone's hopes up. Least of all, her own. She was no stranger to disappointment.

"The man wants to marry you, *schweschder*. I think that's a pretty big thing."

"*Jah*, but I don't know him. How can I even consider something like that? I just...I wish I knew who he was. It's kind of awkward that he knows me and what I look like and I'm over here in the dark. It's not really fair, you know?"

"Maybe he wants you to fall in love with him as a person and not his face. I know the reason I agreed to a courtship with Andy Stoltzfus was because I thought he was handsome. But I felt like we didn't really have that much in common."

Anne shook out one of *Dat's* shirts. "I don't see how. You love books and he's a schoolteacher."

"Well, he wasn't then. And he would never be interested in the books *I* read." Charlotte laughed and shook her head. "I couldn't even imagine. Andy's very quiet and serious."

Anne's lips pressed together. "That's not a bad thing." She admired a thoughtful man.

"*Nee*. We were just too different. And, of course, once Glen came back..."

"I never knew you had a crush on Glen back when we were younger." Anne eyed her *schweschder*.

"It was just a small crush. I realized that I liked him that one time he brought me home from a singing. We'd never courted or kissed or anything back then. I thought he was way too old for me, and I'm sure he didn't see me that way."

"Well, *jah*. Sammy would have had something to say about that. That was when they were having their squabble. But it ended up with Sammy discovering Bertie, so it all worked out." Anne clipped the last item to the line and carried the basket up the stairs.

Charlotte followed.

Anne sighed. If only another letter would come soon. Or, better yet, maybe she could find a *gut* reason to stop by the schoolhouse.

She gave her head a hard shake. *Ach*, what was wrong with her?

CHAPTER 6

If Andy admitted it to himself, he'd acknowledge that the thought of courting an older woman was somewhat intimidating. His cousin Johnny had been three years older than him, and just a year older than Anne. Add that to the fact that women tended to mature faster than men.

Would she even be interested in someone younger, or would she consider him young and immature? In his experience, most men sought out younger women. And that had been true with him and Charlotte. But there was no rule that the man had to be older, was there?

Ach, he hadn't been this nervous in a long time. And he didn't even intend to ask Anne about courting.

Although the ground had cleared of snow, the

weather had been chilly as of late and his hands felt clammy as he held the reins. He inhaled a deep breath. This was only a short trip to his scholars' home, not a stepping out with their older *schweschder*. But, goodness, it sure felt like it was.

Perhaps he shouldn't have donned his for-*gut* clothes. But he'd wanted to look his best for Anne. His eyes shuttered closed. *Gott, please let this go well.*

As soon as he pulled up, he spotted Anne carrying a basket from the hen house. *Ach*, were they still getting eggs yet? *Mamm* had said hers had stopped laying a couple months ago. Perhaps the Eichers had a different breed.

She stopped her trek toward the house and pivoted toward Andy's buggy. His heart pounded harder with each step that brought her closer.

"Andy. This is a surprise." A small smile brightened her face.

He rubbed the back of his neck. "Uh, *jah*. I, um, talked to my *mamm*."

"Your *mamm*?" Her lips twisted and he got the feeling she was confused.

"About the gingersnaps?"

"*Ach, jah*. I remember." She glanced toward the *dawdi haus* where Charlotte had stepped outside.

Andy frowned and lowered his voice. "I have something else to discuss too. Could you, uh, *kumm* for a short ride?"

Anne looked down at her basket of eggs. "Sure. Let me just put this inside and get my coat and gloves."

His pulse pounded as he scrambled for what else they would discuss besides his *mamm*. He needed to come up with something *gut* and quick. When his eyes darted toward the *dawdi haus*, he noticed Charlotte had gone back inside.

"I'm ready." Anne hadn't taken but a moment before reappearing at his buggy.

Ach, he should have gotten out to help her up, but it was too late now.

"I have a quilt in case you need it." He reached over the seat between them and pulled out the warm flannel-backed blanket.

She pulled it around herself. "*Denki*."

"Will Tuesday at nine work for you? *Mamm* said either Tuesday or Thursday. But I thought the sooner we get our cookies, the better."

The comment coaxed a beautiful smile from her lips. But he should not be thinking about her lips. "*Jah*, Tuesday sounds *gut*."

He turned onto the road that led to his property. If only he could summon the courage to ask to court her. But it seemed too soon. And he'd rather be patient than have her reject the idea outright. *Nee*, he would wait.

"Where are we going?"

"*Ach*, nowhere in particular. My property is this way. Have you seen it?"

"*Nee*, I haven't."

They drove in comfortable silence for a few minutes.

"Would you...like to? I've been working on the house in my spare time."

"*Jah*. Sure, I guess." She shrugged.

"Okay." A few minutes later, he pulled into his long driveway.

"This is nice." She seemed to take in their surroundings. "I love the long driveway and the way the trees line up on the side."

"There's some wooded acreage out behind the house too." He pointed to his roughly framed structure. "Unfortunately, I haven't made much progress on it yet. But I got the foundation down a few months ago and just recently framed the outside."

He guided his mare to the hitching post and hopped down.

She nodded and took his hand as he helped her to the ground. Had it been his imagination, or had there been a spark in her eyes?

"What's next?" she asked, while he secured the horse.

They strolled toward the structure. "I ordered the

windows. They should be here this week. I'll install those, then hopefully get the roof up and the siding on. Once that is all done and the doors are installed, it'll be pretty much closed in, and I can start on the inside."

He gestured for her to step inside, then he followed.

"What do you have in mind?"

He explained the layout of the house, complete with his idea for a wraparound porch.

She seemed pleased. "It sounds really nice, Andy."

"I think it will be. I'm just glad the bishop allowed me to keep the camper here. That way, I just come here after school to work when I can."

Her eyebrows lowered. "You're living out here now?"

"*Jah.*" He pointed to the small RV. "Would you like to see inside?"

"*Ach, jah.*" Her smile grew. "I've never seen the inside of one."

He remembered how excited he was when he first saw the inside of his travel trailer. He been amazed so much could fit in something so small.

He opened the door and gestured for her to step inside before him.

"Ah." She gasped. "It's like a little house!" She moved further inside.

"There's a bedroom in the front." He led the way and opened the sliding accordion door. "Sorry my bed's not made." He grimaced.

He hadn't had any intention of bringing a *maedel* into his trailer. Or on his property, for that matter. Her being here was a wonderful *gut* treat.

"That's fine. Your *mamm's* not here." She teased.

"*Nee*, she isn't." He chuckled. "And there's..."

He led the way to the opposite end and attempted to squeeze past her. As he did, their eyes met and held, and she swallowed, the brush of their bodies bringing a zing of warmth clear up to his ears.

"*Ach*, sorry." He'd said the words to be polite, but they were far from the truth.

He recovered, as though his world hadn't just been kicked out of orbit. "There's a small bathroom here. And that table makes into a bed. I think the man I bought it from said six people can sleep inside. More if some sleep on the floor."

Wonder filled her entire face. "That's amazing."

"Well, I guess I should get you back home."

"When will the house be done?"

Andy led the way out of the trailer. "I'm thinking summer, when I have more daylight to work on it."

"Is anyone helping you?"

"Not right now." He untethered the horse.

"You could ask either of my brothers, Sammy or Clive. They might be willing to help once in a while."

He noted that she hadn't mentioned her brother-in-law, Glen. "That would be nice to have some help."

He offered a hand up into his carriage.

"*Denki* for showing me your place. It's going to be really nice."

"I hope so." He stepped into the buggy and began guiding the horse out of the driveway.

A frown tugged her lips downward. "Andy?"

He swallowed, unsure of what her next words might be. *I'm not interested in you. You shouldn't have brought me out here. I'm still in love with Johnny.*

"*Jah*?"

"I just wanted to say that I'm awful sorry for the way my *schweschder* treated you. You're a *gut* guy and you deserve better. I feel terrible about that." She shook her head.

"You shouldn't feel bad because it had nothing to do with you. And to be honest, I don't think Charlotte and I were right for each other. It hurt something wonderful at first. But I've come through it a better man, I think." He stayed close to the edge of the road, allowing a vehicle to pass.

"That's *gut*."

"And what about my cousin Johnny? He did you wrong. I don't know how he could ever..." *Ach*, he was about to say too much. "You didn't deserve that, either."

"Like I said, Johnny and I probably shouldn't have courted as long as we did." She shrugged. "I guess we just got comfortable with each other."

"I reckon *Gott* has a reason for allowing things as He does. His ways are not our ways."

Her face brightened. "*Jah*, that's kind of what the Bible says. That all things work together for *gut* for His people."

"It makes you wonder, doesn't it?" Andy glanced her way, glad to be having this conversation.

"About *Gott*?"

"Oh, I don't know. All of it. Everything that happens in our lives. We're so sure that we want to go one way, but that's not the way *Gott* wants us to go. But we're too stubborn to see it and keep going our own way. Then when the carpet is pulled from under our feet, only then can we see that we were headed the wrong way." He looked at her and scrunched up his face. "Does that make any sense?"

"I think it makes perfect sense. *Gott* had to break me and Johnny up so I could see that we were never right for each other. Same thing with you and Charlotte, I reckon."

"Right." He thought about going one step further and pointing out the fact that *Gott* probably had someone else in mind for them to marry, but that would be too forward.

And just like that, they arrived back at the Eichers' place.

"Home already, I guess." Her look was bittersweet.

"*Denki* for coming with me."

"I...I had a *gut* time, Andy." A becoming blush splashed across her face.

"*Jah*, me too."

"Would you...like to stay for supper?"

Would he? *Ach*, that would be a dream. But he didn't want to wear out his welcome. Besides, what if Charlotte and Glen were there? And how would the *kinner* take to having their new teacher over to supper? That would just be awkward. "I better not. *Denki* for the offer, though."

"Sure." A look of disappointment flashed across her features.

Ach, the last thing he wanted was to disappoint Anne Eicher. He lifted an eyebrow and managed a half smile. "Maybe next time?"

She nodded. "Well, I guess I should go prepare something. No doubt the *kinner* think they've been abandoned."

"*Guten nacht*, Anne." He jiggled the reins as she trotted toward the house.

Andy couldn't help the whistle on his lips as he

traveled home. This had been the best day he'd had in a long time.

CHAPTER 7

The moment Anne stepped inside the house, Charlotte dragged her to the nearest empty bedroom.

"Wait! Did I just see you getting out of Andy Stoltzfus's buggy?" Charlotte bounced on her toes like little Grace did when she was about to get candy.

"Don't make more of it than it is. We were just talking about something we'd discussed at the schoolhouse and didn't want an audience." Anne calmly explained, but her traitorous heart beat wildly.

"Uh-huh. I saw the way he was looking at you."

Anne gasped. "What way?"

Charlotte shrugged. "Like a man in love."

"That's totally ridiculous, Char!"

"What did you two talk about?"

"Making cookies."

"You went on a buggy ride to talk about making cookies?" Charlotte giggled. "*Jah*, he's definitely smitten."

"You're imagining things, *schweschder*."

"We'll see."

"I don't imagine I'll ever go on a buggy ride with him again, so you can lay your silly fantasies to rest."

"Well, then, I guess you'll still want to read this." Charlotte waved a large envelope in front of Anne's face. "It's from your secret admirer." She sang the words in typical Charlotte fashion.

Anne snatched the envelope and pressed it between her fingers. There appeared to be more than just a letter inside. "Excuse me, I have to go start on supper."

Charlotte laughed. "You're not fooling me. You're going to tear that open the moment you step into your room."

Anne shook her head. "I'm saving it until after supper. Are you, Glen, and Grace joining us tonight?"

"No. I made tacos. Those are Glen's favorite."

Suddenly, Anne wondered what her secret admirer's favorite food was. She couldn't wait for supper to be over.

Dear Anne,

I realize you probably weren't expecting this letter yet, but I couldn't help myself from responding to yours.

Anyhow, about what I've enclosed:

I recently brought an order to a store at the mall and the woman there asked if I did commissioned work. When I said yes, she explained what she wanted, and I've enclosed what I came up with. It's a Christmas ornament. I know we don't typically have Christmas trees, but I had this one left over and I just felt Der Herr prompting me to send it to you. Anyway, I hope you like it.

ANNE UNFOLDED THE TISSUE PAPER, feeling something sturdy between her fingers. Her breath caught the moment the miniature nativity—a silhouette of Joseph, Mary, and Baby Jesus—slipped out of its wrapping and into her hand. *Ach*, he'd made this beautiful work of art?

She imagined an Amish man near her own age, shoulders broad with strong arms and hands capable of the intricate details of the ornament she held.

A sudden image of Jane and Zane's teacher flashed in her mind. His smiling eyes intriguing yet shy. *Ach*, this was Andrew Stoltzfus, her *schweschder's* former beau and Johnny's cousin she was thinking about. It was completely ridiculous. How had he crept into her mind? She blamed it on Charlotte and her fanciful thoughts.

She shook away the image. It was impossible that the letter writer was Andrew. He lived here in Indiana, not in Ohio. And he was a teacher, not a woodworker. Not to mention he'd been working on his house. He wouldn't have time to do all of those things, would he?

Her thoughts were completely ridiculous, so she shoved them from her mind. Her eyes trained on the letter again.

Wow! It sounds like you are busy. I'm sorry about your mother. It must've been hard to not only lose her but to assume most of her responsibilities at sixteen. Change can be hard sometimes, but I know God helps us through.

About your cookie question: Let's just say that I've never met a cookie that I didn't like! I'd imagine any cookie you might bake would be delicious.

Until next time,
Your secret friend

ANNE SIGHED as she closed the letter. If this *was* indeed Andy Stoltzfus, he was being quite clever. She stared down at the small Christmas ornament then clasped it to her heart. Whoever this man was, he was thoughtful.

He'd mentioned *Der Herr* once again, which led her to believe that he wasn't someone who regarded *Gott* casually but believed and actually applied His Word.

Like *Dat*.

She wasn't worldly wise by any means, but she'd lived long enough to know that a faith like that was valuable and rare.

Secret Friend, I just might be falling for you.

CHAPTER 8

Although Andy spent a lot of his time in the camper on his property, he traveled back and forth to his and Johnny's apartment in Ohio and occasionally stayed the night there. He'd promised Johnny he'd still pay for half the rent for as long as he kept his personal belongings there, or basically, until his house was ready to be moved into, which seemed like a long time coming at the rate he'd been going.

Johnny had settled into the *Englisch* lifestyle and had been taking classes at the local college, so they pretty much lived separate lives. Occasionally, they'd be home at the same time and share a meal together.

If Andy admitted it, sometimes Johnny got on his nerves, and he preferred the times when he could enjoy some peace and quiet. Johnny always wanted the radio or the television on when he was home. It was one of the reasons Andy was anxious to get his house completed.

He looked forward to spring and summer when he'd have more daylight hours to work on the house. But the thought of making Anne Eicher his *fraa* and moving in there with her ignited a fire in him like nothing else. Taking her by his property had been a spur of the moment thing, and he was a little surprised that she'd agreed.

And then, there was that moment in the trailer. He'd never felt like kissing anyone more than in that moment, but he'd managed to refrain. He often wondered how she would have responded. Would she have pushed him away? Would she have been disgusted? Would she have kissed him back?

He sighed.

Now, he sat at his desk contemplating what he'd write to her in his next letter. He hoped she liked the Christmas ornament he'd enclosed in the last one.

Johnny appeared out of nowhere and snatched the envelope that held Anne's last letter from Andy's desk. "Hey, what is this?"

Andy reached for the letter, but Johnny moved further away.

"Give it back, please."

Johnny examined the letter again. "This is Anne's

handwriting. What is she doing writing to *you*? You have a box at the post office?"

Andy's lips pressed together in a hard line. He hadn't wanted anyone to know. Especially Johnny.

"Wait." Johnny scowled. "Are you writing *love* letters to my *aldi*?"

"She's not your *aldi* anymore."

Fire flashed in his eyes. "Like heck she isn't."

Andy's eyes flew wide. "What do you mean? It's been months since you've even seen her. You said you weren't going back to the Amish. I highly doubt Anne has any aspirations of leaving."

"I could persuade her." Johnny's eyes sparkled with mischief.

Uneasiness grew in the pit of Andy's stomach. "She won't leave her family."

"Don't be so sure about that."

"I am sure. She's told me as much."

Johnny's arms jammed across his chest. "Are you courting her?"

"What if I am?" Heat crawled up his neck.

"Seriously, cousin? You make a move on my girl the second I'm out of the picture? What gives, man?"

He was tempted to tell Johnny that he didn't deserve a woman like Anne, but that would only make his cousin's anger flare more. "If you truly cared about her, the two of you would have been married years ago.

You don't string a woman along all that time and expect her to wait forever for you to make up your mind. No woman deserves to be treated that way."

"So now you're going to tell me how to treat women?" Johnny huffed.

Andy finally secured the letter. "Let's just forget about this, okay? She doesn't even know it's me, anyhow."

Johnny's forehead wrinkled. "What do you mean by that?"

"I mean that I'm writing to her anonymously."

Johnny tossed his head back and howled with laughter. Andy didn't find his situation funny in the least.

His cousin finally found his breath. "You have got to be kidding me." Johnny's eyes narrowed. "Are you in love with her?"

Andy palmed his eyes. He really did not want to discuss this with anyone, especially with Anne's former beau. "I don't know."

Johnny shook his head. "I'm not sure how I feel about all this, cousin."

"Whatever you do, please don't tell her it's me."

"Why? Afraid she'll drop you like a hot potato?" Johnny snickered. "Like her *schweschder* did?"

That was a low blow, even for Johnny. "Come on, man."

"Alright. Alright." He held up both hands. "I won't tell her it's you. Not that I'm going to see her anyhow."

Andy blew out a relieved breath.

But he couldn't help but wonder now. Did his cousin still have feelings for Anne?

CHAPTER 9

Later in the week, Charlotte, Glen, and little Grace joined the Eicher family for supper. Although Anne's and Charlotte's personalities were like night and day, Anne felt like Charlotte was her closest friend and confidant. When *Mamm* was alive, she had filled that role.

Now that supper was over, the two of them quietly worked together in the kitchen as the others lounged in the living room, reading and playing games.

"Does Andy Stoltzfus do woodwork?" Anne attempted to sound casual as she placed the clean dish in the cupboard.

Charlotte frowned. "Woodwork? Andy? Not that I know of." A look flashed across her face. And here it came. "Why?"

She shrugged. "Just curious."

"Hmm..." Charlotte's eyes sparkled. "It wonders me if my *schweschder* might be interested in Andy Stoltzfus?"

"Goodness, Char. I just asked a question." Her brow lowered. "Besides, wouldn't that be awkward? For you and Glen, especially?"

Charlotte shook her head. "*Nee*. Andy's a great guy. I'm sorry for hurting him the way we did. I went about our relationship the wrong way."

"Have you ever apologized?" She remembered the hurt in Andy's eyes the day he left.

"*Ach*, just at the bridge when he found me and Glen there. Probably wasn't the best timing." She frowned. "Now that he's back, maybe I should talk to him. Clear the air between us."

Anne grinned. "And you think *Glen* will be fine with that?" Her *schweschder's* husband tended to have a bit of a jealous streak when it came to her *schweschder* and other men. Especially her former beau.

Charlotte shrugged. "He'll have to be."

"You could just write him a note and send it with Zane."

"And take the chance of it falling into the wrong hands? No way." Charlotte grimaced. "Glen will just have to deal with it."

Glen chose that moment to make an appearance. "I'll have to deal with what?"

Charlotte's arms jammed across her chest. "Were you eavesdropping on us, husband?"

"*Nee*. Just came in for a drink." He leaned in and claimed a kiss from his *fraa*. "Now, what's this about me dealing with something?"

"I need to apologize to Andy. In person."

Glen scowled and shook his head. "You already did that."

"That didn't count, and you know it."

Glen's lips pressed together. "I don't like it. What if he tries to put the moves on you?"

Charlotte snorted. "Put the moves on me—a married woman? I think you listened to too much of that crazy music when you were *Englisch*." She shook her head.

"I think the both of you should go and apologize to Andy Stoltzfus." All three of them turned at the sound of Sammy's voice.

"Sammy. I didn't know you were coming by." Anne's grin stretched across her face, always happy to see her oldest *bruder*. They'd been worried about him a few years ago. After *Mamm* died, Sammy hadn't taken it well. He'd ventured into the *Englisch* world and gotten himself into all kinds of trouble. Fortunately, *Der Herr* had helped him see the error of his ways, and with a little prompting from *Dat* and Bertie, he'd rejoined the community.

Sammy shrugged. "*Chust* stopped in for a minute. You got any goodies I can take back for *mei fraa*?" He winked.

"You can take some cookies." Anne offered a plate of her latest batch.

"*Denki*. I'm going to say hello to *Dat* and everyone real quick before I go." Sammy turned and pointed at his best friend-turned-brother-in-law. "Seriously, though, Glen. You should make things right with Andy Stoltzfus. You both did him wrong. Not *chust mei schweschder*."

Glen frowned. "I hate it when you're right."

Sammy lifted a cocky grin. "*Jah*, I know." Then he slipped from the room.

They all chuckled at Sammy's parting gesture. *Ach*, it felt like the world had been set back to rights when her *bruder* had returned. Anne would never cease to thank *Der Herr* for that blessing.

"Besides, you don't need to worry, *schatzi*. I heard it through the grapevine that Teacher Andrew already has someone." Charlotte picked back up where their previous conversation had ended.

Something squeezed inside Anne's chest at Charlotte's words. She hadn't considered that Andrew might have already moved on and found another *aldi*.

Glen's countenance relaxed. "Really?"

"If Zane's words were true."

"What did Zane say?" Anne's curiosity was piqued now.

"He said Andy's *schweschder* said that he's courting someone." Charlotte's eyebrows moved up a half inch.

"*Ach.*" Anne's eyes slid to Glen.

Charlotte got the message and shooed her husband out of the kitchen. She turned back to Anne. "What was that look for?"

"I probably shouldn't have agreed to ride with him the other day, then." Anne nibbled on her fingernail. "Now, I feel bad."

"Unless the one he said he was courting was you."

"That's quite a *ferhoodled* notion, even for you, *schweschder.*" Anne laughed out loud. "I've never known Andrew Stoltzfus to be a liar. Have you?"

"*Nee.*" Charlotte's lips twisted. "Why'd you ask about the woodworking?"

Anne pulled the Christmas ornament from her apron pocket and showed Charlotte.

Her *schweschder* gasped. "Did he give this to you?"

"The secret letter writer did, *jah*. Said he made it."

Charlotte shook her head. "If it was Andy, don't you think he would have given me one of his creations while we were courting? Surely, I would have at least known that he made stuff like this."

"That's what I was thinking." Something about that made her sad.

"Were you thinking the letter writer could be him?"

Anne shrugged. "I don't know. They just kind of remind me of each other sometimes."

"I really like this." Charlotte's fingers moved over the ornament. "Does he sell them?"

"I think so. *Jah*, he said that he did at the shopping mall."

"Interesting..."

"What are you thinking?" Anne examined her *schweschder*.

"What if you and I took a little trip?"

"Where?"

"To the mall."

Anne laughed. "He's in Ohio. There must be hundreds of malls there. And who knows how many stores inside the mall. It would be like looking for a needle in a haystack."

"*Jah*, you're probably right." Charlotte's excitement deflated. "But what if we went to the mall closest to the post office where his letter was sent from? Why not? It would be fun, anyhow. And we could maybe find a Christmas gift or two at the mall."

"You want to give something store-bought?" For some reason, the idea brought a touch of sadness.

"You don't like the idea?"

Anne shrugged. "I just feel like it's much more

meaningful if a gift is something that you've made. Something that comes from your heart."

"Kind of like this Christmas ornament?" Charlotte's eyes twinkled.

"Exactly."

"I CAN'T BELIEVE I let you talk me into this." Anne's eyes darted around, taking in all the activity as shoppers went in and out of the various mall shops.

Soft but cheery Christmas music played in the background, sending a happy feeling through her and making her long to go caroling again like their youth group had done in the past years.

"Do you ever miss caroling?" Anne blurted her thoughts. She tended to do that when around her *schweschder*. Charlotte's free-spirited personality sometimes rubbed off.

"*Ach*, yes! You can still go, you know? Glen and I even went last year when our group visited the list of folks Bishop Omar gave us. We might go again this year."

Anne thought about the joy that sparked on the faces of those whom they usually visited. Her mind went back to the blessing box. Maybe she'd suggest the recipients' names to the bishop this year in case he didn't already have them on the list.

She wondered if Andy would take part in caroling this year.

"This is going to be so much fun!" Charlotte's bright eyes reflected her wide grin as she eyed the stores. "Now, keep your eyes open for a Christmas tree."

Anne laughed. "I think there might be a Christmas tree in every store here."

"Look, there!" Charlotte pointed to a large tree in the center of the mall. She grasped Anne's hand and pulled her along. "Let's go see."

The moment they arrived at the tree, Anne noticed an ornament identical to the one her secret letter writer sent. "It's here!"

Charlotte beamed. "I knew it." She looked around the tree and they spotted several more.

Anne noticed a woman sitting behind a counter. Her eyes took in the sign that appeared to be for some charity. "What is this?" She asked the woman.

"This is our annual Christmas drive." She gestured toward the tree. "Donors get to take one of those ornaments from the tree as a thank-you for donating gifts for families in need."

Charlotte moved to the counter. "Where did the ornaments come from?"

The woman smiled. "They're from an anonymous donor. Very generous. This time of year seems to bring out the best in people."

Anonymous, indeed.

"Are they for sale anywhere?" Charlotte asked.

"I'm not sure. You can check the stores." The lady seemed disappointed. "Or you can donate a gift and get one for free."

Anne and Charlotte exchanged glances.

"We'll see if we can find something." Anne smiled. She didn't intend on taking one of the ornaments since she already had one, but helping out a needy family is something she'd love to do.

She and Charlotte ventured into various stores, but nothing specific caught their eye.

Charlotte pulled her into a bookstore. "I found it! Goodness, Anne. Is this perfect or what?"

It took Anne a moment to see what had caught her *schweschder's* eye.

"Look! It's Raggedy Ann and Andy. One of my favorites." Charlotte held out a book and a set of dolls.

Anne laughed out loud.

Charlotte studied her. "What?"

"Anne and Andy." Her eyes lit up at the humor in it. What were the odds?

Charlotte grasped Anne's upper arm and shook

her. Her smile took over her entire face. "This is a sign. Anne and Andy."

Anne shook her head. "Don't be *narrisch, schweschder*. It's just a happy coincidence."

"*Dat* says there's no such thing as coincidences." Charlotte nodded matter-of-factly. "We're getting this."

As Anne and Charlotte traveled back home, Anne couldn't help but wonder if her *schweschder's* words held merit. Had the dolls been a sign that she and Andy were meant to be together? *Nee*, she didn't believe in all that nonsense.

But still, she couldn't help but wonder...

CHAPTER 10

The buggy rolled to a stop. Anne had to admit she was a little nervous showing up at the Stoltzfus's home.

But that apprehension quickly dissipated a few moments after Andy's *mamm* welcomed her inside with open arms.

"I can't tell you how many times in the last week Andrew has mentioned you coming over." Rose Stoltzfus said as she released Anne from her embrace.

"He sure does love his cookies, doesn't he?" Anne smiled.

"That, he does. But, between you and me, I've never seen that *bu this* excited about cookies." She winked, moving into the kitchen.

Ach, what had she meant by that?

"I never thought that *bu* would recover after what happened with your *schweschder*, but I for one, am wonderful glad to see that sparkle back in his eye."

"Oh. Well, we're not—"

"You don't need to explain anything to me, *liebling*." Rose patted her hand. "You know what they say, nothing is fair in love and war."

Anne suppressed a smile. She was pretty sure that wasn't how the phrase went or how it applied to their situation. But she wouldn't ask what Rose meant by that.

"But now that your *schweschder* is married to that Kauffman *bu*, and that *dummkopp* Johnny Hershberger jumped the fence to the *Englisch*, I'd say you're both fair game."

Oh, dear.

Perhaps she should set Andy's *mamm* straight on their relationship. And, although Johnny had left, there was still a tender place in her heart for her former beau. After all, they'd dated over five years. Goodness, she'd never known anyone to speak so frankly.

Rose hefted a tin container marked "flour" from the cupboard and one marked "sugar" and plunked them onto the kitchen table. "I know. I know. He's *mei schweschder's bu*. I should be more charitable. But he certainly has some growing up to do. Selfish *bu*, that one is. Always has been. Opposite of my Andy. Don't know how those two ever ended up becoming best friends."

Ach, she needed to try and change the subject. "My *schweschder* and I are opposite too, and I consider her my best friend."

"She's a *gut maedel*, just couldn't make up her mind. Glad she finally settled. I hope they can make it work. It's quite risky marrying an *Englischer*. Nothing against her, but I never thought she was right for Andy. Maybe it was just a *mudder's* knowing, but something was off with those two."

"Glen Kauffman and his *dochder* are Amish now."

"You know what they say. What's *gut* for the cat isn't always *gut* for the kittens."

Anne suppressed a chuckle. Andy's *mudder* certainly was a different kind of person. Anne loved her immediately, but she had no idea what Rose meant by these sayings.

"Do you have a recipe for the cookies? Do we have everything we need?" Anne surveyed the contents on the counter. Flour, sugar, molasses, cinnamon, ginger, cayenne...

Wait. Cayenne?

"I see you eyeing my special spices." Rose grinned with her entire face and held up the cayenne. "*This* is the secret to the perfect gingersnap. Not too much, though, or not even the dog will eat them. *Kumm, maedel.* I will show you how. Easier than pie on a Sunday afternoon." She winked.

Anne gasped. They'd never been allowed to prepare pies on *Der Herr's* day. "A Sunday afternoon?"

"Now, before you start thinking I'm committing sacrilege, I don't *bake* my pies on Sunday. I only *serve* them then. That's why it's easy."

Ach, finally one of her sayings made sense. Sort of.

TRUTH BE TOLD, Andy had been worried all day about Anne meeting with *Mamm* to make cookies.

The main reason he'd suggested it in the first place was because he thought he'd be spending time with Anne in the kitchen.

Visions had filled his head of the two of them. Having fun. Teasing each other. Making a mess of themselves. Seeing her eyes sparkle. Maybe even sharing a kiss.

He loved his *mamm*. Truly, he did. But *Gott* only knew what kind of stories about him she'd be sharing with Anne. Although he'd made sure his *mamm* understood that they weren't courting, he'd seen the twinkle in her eye.

If he had to guess, *Mamm* was likely highlighting

all of Andy's *gut* qualities. And sharing her "sayings" that nobody understood but her.

Ach, this was going to be a disaster.

CHAPTER 11

Andy glanced up at the clock and sighed.

Three thirty. The scholars had been let out an hour ago. Surely *Mamm* and Anne were finished with the cookies by now. They'd planned to meet in the morning.

Anne had said she'd bring cookies by the schoolhouse when they were done, hadn't she? So, why hadn't she shown up yet? Did she think he'd gone to the trailer already? Did she forget and decide to go home?

Or even worse, was she held up by *Mamm*? When *Mamm* got to talking, sometimes it was hard to slip away. Anne was likely too polite to cut *Mamm* off. Now that he thought about it, that was likely the case.

Ach, perhaps he should go rescue her.

He hitched the buggy to the horse in record time.

Fortunately, his folks' place was only a couple of miles from the schoolhouse.

The moment he pulled into the driveway, his lips tugged downward. Anne's carriage was nowhere to be found.

His younger brother careened out of the house and down the steps and rushed toward Andy's buggy. *Gut*. If he could get an answer from his *bruder*, he wouldn't have to waste precious time by going inside. Then *he* would be the one held up by *Mamm*. Not that he minded, but he was on a mission right now.

"Is Anne Eicher inside with *Mamm*?"

His *bruder's* lips turned sideways. "Ain't no Eichers here."

"Zane and Jane's *schweschder* isn't here?" He clarified just so his *bruder* understood

"*Nee*."

"*Allrecht*. Tell *Mamm* I'll be over on Friday for supper." He waved goodbye to his *bruder* and set off for his trailer. He'd thought about going by the Eichers' but he didn't want to make a pest of himself or seem overeager. Which he admitted to himself that he was.

He sighed. Perhaps Anne would bring the cookies by the schoolhouse tomorrow instead. He shook his head. That was a silly thought. If anything, she'd just send them to school with the *kinner*.

Ach, he'd been sure she would show up at the schoolhouse. He'd been imagining her beautiful smile all day. He'd found himself wishing someone responsible would show up, so he could take a quick break and drop in on them while they were making cookies. But, alas, it wasn't to be.

ANNE TURNED at the sound of buggy wheels crunching on the half-dirt-half-gravel road.

Gut.

She'd been worried Andy wouldn't show up and she'd have to leave his gingersnaps on the trailer steps. She'd knocked on the door and when no one answered, she tried the handle. To her surprise, it had come open. She called into the trailer but there was no answer.

To go inside and set the cookies on the table, albeit tempting, would have felt like invading his privacy so she'd decided just to leave them outside and hope the wild animals wouldn't get to them.

But none of that mattered now.

Andy hopped down from the buggy and tethered his horse to the hitching post in what seemed like record speed. "*Ach*, I didn't expect you to be here."

Was that pleasure in his eyes?

"I would have stopped by the schoolhouse, but I had to go home first to thaw out some chicken. I forgot to take it out of the icebox this morning before I left for your *mamm's*."

His color seemed to darken at the mention of his *mamm*. "I'm afraid to ask. How did it go?"

She couldn't help the laugh that slipped from her lips. "It was...interesting."

They walked toward the trailer.

"That's what I was afraid of." He grimaced. "Was she trying to matchmake again?"

Anne picked up the cookies from the steps. "She did mention you on occasion. All *gut* things, mind you."

"*Jah*, I'm sure of that." He shook his head. "I'm sorry."

"Oh, don't be. I enjoyed her company. And learned a few tips on how to make gingersnaps." As she handed over the plate, his fingers covered hers, sending a rush of heat all the way up her neck.

"*Denki*." His voice was low, and his gaze conveyed gratitude. "This means a lot."

She swallowed, not able to break their connection. "It does?"

"Would you, uh, like to come inside and help me taste test these?" She saw the tease in his eye.

His offer was so tempting. "I...I should probably

get back." She gestured toward her buggy. "You know, supper and all."

"Are you sure you can't stay a couple of minutes?" She caught the longing in his voice. "I just bought a fresh jar of milk."

What would it hurt to spend a few extra minutes with this kind, handsome man? "*Ach*, who can say no to milk and cookies?"

His smile filled his entire face. "*Wunderbaar*."

AFTER TURNING up the propane heater, Andy snatched the only two cups he owned from the cupboard and set them on his tiny counter. He cursed his shaking hand as he poured the milk with care, thankful his back was turned to Anne.

He placed a cup of milk in front of her and sat down opposite her at his small table. Their knees brushed, then he repositioned his legs. The last thing he wanted to do was seem too forward and scare her off.

"*Denki*." She took a sip and removed the foil from the plate of cookies.

"My pleasure." He reached for a gingersnap. "Now let's see if these are any *gut*." He winked, then sank his teeth into the cookie.

She rubbed her hands in what could only be anticipation.

True to form, the cookie had just the right amount of snap to it. He closed his eyes as the flavors mingled in his mouth. "Mm...it's delicious. The right amount of snap and apparently just the right amount of everything else too. *Gut* job. I think this is the best one I've had yet."

"Truly?" Her eyes lit with excitement, then she took a cookie for herself.

"Without a doubt. The spice is perfect." He groaned in pleasure.

Color rose to her cheeks as she watched him eat. She pulled her eyes away and surveyed the small space. "What do you plan to do with this once your house is built?"

"I'll need to sell it. That was one of the conditions of being able to buy it in the first place."

She took a sip of milk to wash down her cookie. "That's too bad. It's so cute. Although, I don't know what use you'd have for it after your house is done."

He snatched another cookie. "I'm sure some *Englisch* family would like to have it for camping. A little home away from home."

She laughed as he popped one more into his mouth. "You really *are* addicted to those, aren't you?"

He patted his stomach. "I'm a growing boy."

"*Ach*, you're hardly a *bu* anymore, Andrew Stoltzfus." Her eyes grew wide, and she ducked her head as though she wished she'd kept the thought to herself.

But he didn't mind one bit. It was *gut* to know she saw him as a man. Perhaps lifting those dumbbells Johnny had insisted on buying was paying off.

"I should go now." Her smile dimmed.

"I'll walk you out." He scooted out of the small bench, then held out his hand to help her from hers. When she came to her full height, they stood just inches from each other. His heart pounded so loud at her nearness, he was almost certain she could hear it too.

His eyes roamed over her face, then he stilled as she reached toward him and brushed crumbs from the edge of his mouth. His lips tingled with her touch. He caught her hand before she could let it fall, unsure what he planned to do with it, yet knowing he couldn't let the opportunity pass.

Her eyes darted from his face to their hands then back to his face again. "I...there was something..."

Her words trailed off as he brought her hand to his mouth and pressed his lips to the back of it. "*Denki* again, Anne." When he freed her hand, she released a sigh as though she'd been holding her breath.

He moved to the door and held it open for her. She descended the trailer steps, then he escorted her to the buggy. He untethered her mare as she stepped into the cab.

"You going to be warm enough?" He handed over the reins.

A shy smile graced her face. "I think I'm plenty warm now, Andy Stoltzfus."

He couldn't hide his grin if he wanted to. "*Gut.*"

He stepped away as she backed up the horse, waved, then set off toward home.

CHAPTER 12

Anne hummed Christmas carols the entire ride home.

She wasn't sure how she'd arrived, though, because her mind had been occupied by a certain schoolteacher. *Ach*, had she been too forward touching him like she had? It had seemed so natural at the time.

And then when he caught her fingers with his, she thought her heart might stop. She was unsure if he would kiss her, and if he did, was that what she wanted? She closed her eyes. *Jah*, she did, she acknowledged to herself. She would welcome Andy Stoltzfus's kiss.

But then he'd only chosen to kiss her hand, which turned out to be nearly as romantic as a lip kiss. By the look in his eyes, she sensed he wanted more but was being cautious. She couldn't fault him for that.

Perhaps she should have encouraged him.

She shook her head at the thought. If she and Andy started courting and she kept sending letters to her secret friend, would that be the same thing as cheating? Because Andy Stoltzfus was the last person who deserved to be cheated on—especially after what happened with Charlotte and Glen.

Of course, she and Andy weren't courting. And as long as they weren't, she could still write to her friend. She hadn't made him any promises, but she didn't want to hurt him either.

Ach, perhaps she should talk to *Dat* or Sammy. *Jah*, Sammy might be a *gut* one to talk to since he experienced what it was like to be cheated on from a man's perspective.

ALTHOUGH GOING BACK to the apartment wasn't Andy's favorite thing, he still traveled there at least once a week. Since he'd been writing to Anne, he always made a point to check his box at least twice a week. There was a secret thrill in knowing that his identity was hidden from her, yet at the same time, he wanted her to know.

If they continued seeing each other and ended up in situations like the one last night, then he'd have to reveal his identity sooner rather than later. He didn't want to put her in an uncomfortable position, although their letter writing had been strictly platonic—at least on her end.

His driver stopped near the apartments parking lot to let him out. He handed over the fare, apologized again for the late hour, said thank you, then headed to their apartment door.

Chances were, Johnny would be asleep already, which suited Andy just fine. He'd enter as quietly as possible. Thankfully, Johnny's bedroom was further down the hall than his so he probably wouldn't even know Andy had come home until morning.

ANDY YAWNED as he threw the covers off himself and stepped onto the carpeted floor. Carpets were something he'd never had living Amish, although they did have throw rugs in various places throughout his folks' house. Just not in his room. So stepping onto a soft warm carpet was a luxury he shouldn't get used to.

But then he thought for a moment. He no longer lived at home. Since he was building his own place, he could put rugs wherever he pleased—even in his bedroom. As far as he knew, there was nothing in the *Ordnung* forbidding it.

Ach, it was exciting being his own man. He hadn't ever thought of little freedoms such as having a rug on the floor next to his bed. Wouldn't that be a treat for his future *fraa*? Which made him wonder, did Anne have a rug beside her bed? Perhaps he'd ask her in his next letter.

Or maybe he'd ask her in person. Would that seem like a weird thing to ask? At least if he asked through a letter, she wouldn't see his neck mottle with redness.

Either way, he needed a shower before beginning his day. He had more orders to craft. He wished he could give something to Anne in person, but then he would definitely give his secret letter writer's identity away.

As he stepped into the shower, he thought about an appropriate gift for Anne. Perhaps she'd like something to do with baking. An apron, maybe?

One thing he was sure of was that it was going to take some fancy footwork to keep both his secret letter personality and his teacher personality separate. He'd already thought about asking her something in a letter, only to remember they'd discussed it in person and the only way he'd be asking the question was because they'd spoken about it.

After he toweled off, he slipped his shorts on, then

headed to their tiny kitchen for a cup of much-needed coffee. After his late night working on the cabin yesterday, he needed the extra jolt of caffeine.

When he entered the dining area, his mouth dropped open. *Ach*, had he come to the wrong apartment? And if not, who in the world was the woman standing in his kitchen? Clad in only a short thin nightdress.

"It's about time you—" Her words cut off as her eyes roamed his face and bare chest. "You're not Johnny."

She immediately picked up a frying pan. "Who are you and what are you doing here?"

He held up both of his hands and glanced over his shoulder for any sign of his cousin. "I think I should ask you the same thing."

"I'm going to give you five seconds to answer before I clobber you with this." She held the pan higher.

"I live here."

"Johnny!" She hollered.

Johnny ran into the room, his boxer shorts and messed hair telling Andy he'd just jumped out of bed.

"What? What's going on?" His eyes went back and forth between Andy and the strange woman standing in the kitchen wielding the frying pan.

"Do you know this guy?" She swung the pan back with both hands.

Johnny shimmied around Andy and disarmed the woman. He set the pan on the counter and sighed. "I forgot you two don't know each other. Stacy, this is my cousin, Andy. Andy, Stacy."

Her jaw dropped. "He said he lives here."

Johnny shook his head. "He kind of lives here sometimes. Right, Andy?"

"I have about a hundred questions right now." Andy frowned at Johnny. "Who is she and why is she here?"

"That's a bit rude, buddy." The woman frowned.

"She's a classmate. She needed a place to stay. I told her she could use our couch until she figures things out."

Andy's hands plowed through his hair. "You told this woman she could live *here*? With us?"

"Wow, this guy has no manners." The woman shook her head.

"Us? You're hardly here, Andy. I didn't let her have your room or anything. What gives, man?"

The woman nodded. "Yeah, what gives?"

"I'll tell you what the problem is. We can't have a woman here. Especially not..." He gestured to her skimpy nightgown. "This isn't right."

"Sheesh. This guy's a square if I've ever seen one." She rolled her eyes.

He held his palms up. "If she's staying here, me and my rent money are leaving. That's all I have to say." He could stay in the trailer full time and check his mailbox when needed.

"Really? You would do that?" Fury burned in Johnny's eyes. "We had an agreement."

"Yes, between you and me." Andy's eyes flicked to the woman then back to Johnny. "The *two* of us."

She pushed through the two of them, grabbed a housecoat from the couch and pulled it around her shoulders, then took something from a purse on the floor beside the couch. "I'm going out for a smoke."

CHAPTER 13

The moment the door clicked behind her, Andy turned to Johnny. "What in the world are you doing bringing a woman here?"

"I already told you." Johnny's hands settled on his hips.

Andy felt his eyes bulging. "Are you...did you share the marriage bed with her?"

Johnny snickered. "She was right, you *are* a square. Come on, Andy. You can't expect me to live Amish out here in the world."

Andy's fists clenched so hard, he was afraid he might do something he and Johnny would both regret. "I can't believe this."

Johnny touched his shoulder. "Chill out, cousin. I didn't sleep with her, okay?"

Andy wasn't sure if he believed him or not. "She can't stay here."

"You're never here. What does it even matter to you?"

"It's wrong. What would Anne think?"

Johnny's arms crossed over his chest. "Oh, I don't know. What *would* she think? You and her seem to be all buddy buddy now."

"Come on, Johnny. Have you even contacted her once since you've been gone? Don't start acting like you care about her now."

Before Andy knew what was happening, Johnny thrust his hands into Andy's shoulders and shoved him against the wall. His finger flew in Andy's face. "I dated her for five years! Of course, I care about her. Do you think it's easy for me to stand back and watch you try to woo her?"

"It's been a few letters." Johnny didn't need to know about their buggy ride or the cookies or the trailer.

"*Jah*, right. You go ahead and tell yourself that, but you and I both know there's a lot more to it than that." Johnny hadn't been spying on them, had he?

"What are you referring to?"

"Do you think I'm stupid? You are clearly head over heels for my girl. Now tell me honestly, have you spent time with her or talked to her other than through the letters?" Johnny stared him down, his features menacing.

Andy's lips pressed together, but he didn't answer.

"*Jah*, that's what I thought. Don't you dare judge *me*."

"What? Did you expect her to wait for you forever?" Andy scowled. "If you had in mind to return to her, maybe you should have let her know."

Johnny shoved past him and bent over the trash can. He pulled out a crumpled piece of paper and thrust it in Andy's face.

"What is this?" Andy scanned Johnny's face for an answer, but he just shook his head.

He opened the paper and immediately noticed Anne's handwriting. Had Johnny stolen this letter from Andy's desk? But no, it was addressed to his cousin. His eyes flew to the words.

Johnny,

My answer is no. I have moved on now, and I consider our relationship over.

Anne

"Now you tell me, Andy. Just *who* has my *aldi moved on* with?"

Andy frowned. "What did you write to her? What was the question?"

"Does it even matter? I might have had a chance if you hadn't butted in. But now, there's no hope."

"Tell me what your letter said." His teeth ground together.

"I told her that I planned to come back. And when I did, I wanted to marry her." Johnny looked away.

Andy's heart clenched. Did his cousin truly want to reconcile with Anne? Because if he did... "*Allrecht*, then..." He shrugged helplessly because he didn't know what else to do. Pressure squeezed inside his chest, but he knew what he had to do. "I guess I'll end things with her. If you truly want her back. If you love her..."

Ach, why did this hurt so much? It wasn't like he'd even asked to court her yet. But their relationship had been progressing so beautifully...

"What? You're just going to step out of the way?" Johnny stared at him now.

"Do you love her or not?"

"*Jah*, I do."

"Well, then who am I to stand in the way? I never would have started this if I would have known you truly still cared for her." He swallowed down the lump in his throat. It would be hard to give her up, but he'd do it for Johnny.

And he didn't want to admit it to himself, but if Anne had stayed with Johnny over five years, then she must've loved him as well. It would likely only take a little spark to kindle that flame again.

CHAPTER 14

Anne sat at her *bruder* Sammy's table sipping the hot apple cider her *schweschder*-in-law, Roberta, had prepared. As the flavors mingled on her tongue, she heard the *boppli* crying in the other room.

"Well." Roberta stood from the table and squeezed Sammy's shoulder. "I guess I'll let you two talk while I change and feed Walt."

"*Denki* for the cider, Bertie." Anne smiled as her *schweschder*-in-law planted a quick kiss on her *bruder's* cheek and exited the room. She studied her brother. "She didn't have to leave the room."

Sammy shrugged. "It's fine. You said you wanted to talk to me?"

"It's about Andy. And the letters that I've been receiving." The words spilled out.

"Andy...? Stoltzfus?"

"*Jah*. Well, we've kind of been spending time together. I think I like him." She huffed a sigh then moved a strand of hair behind her ear. "But I've been writing to this other person who likes me too. And I think I might like him, but I don't know who he is."

Sammy rubbed his temples. "*Kumm* again?"

"I think I like two people, and I don't know what to do about it."

"Are you talking about the secret letter guy?" Sammy's eyebrow inched upward.

"*Jah*." She nodded.

"And Andy Stoltzfus?"

"Right."

Sammy's finger moved along the edge of his mug. "Does Charlotte know about you and Andy?"

"Kind of." She tugged her lip between her teeth. "She suspects as much."

"And Glen?"

"I don't know about Glen." She shook her head. "Do you think he'd have a problem with Andy?"

Sammy swatted the air in front of him. "*Ach*, he'll get over it. I had to when Glen came back. Besides, he wasn't the one who was done wrong by our *schweschder*. Andy was. So, I think that gives Andy more say-so in this matter than Glen."

"Right."

"So, am I hearing you right? You're choosing Andy and you're going to cut things off with the secret letter guy?"

"What do you think I should do?"

"*Ach*, it's your choice so I can't really say one way or another. But the Bible says a double-minded man is unstable in all his ways. So, pick one or the other and stick with your choice."

"If I choose Andy, do you think I should tell him about the letters?"

Sammy gulped down the remainder of his cider. "If you want, but I don't think it's necessary since you haven't really committed yourself in any way. Just so long as you cut things off immediately."

"I just feel like either way someone is going to get hurt."

"It might be inevitable at this point. But sooner rather than later, *ain't not*?" He reached over the table and squeezed her hand. "By the way, Andy's a *gut* guy. I think he'd be a *gut* choice. And since you don't know who the letter person is, well..." Sammy shrugged. "I guess it's his loss."

"I don't know, but I kind of had a feeling they might be one and the same. But I don't know for sure and certain. It's just a hunch I have."

Sammy grinned. "Well, in that case, you don't even need to worry about hurting anyone, do you?"

"*Ach*, I guess not. Maybe I'm worrying about nothing."

ANDY TOSSED and turned the entire night.

He'd be useless for school this morning if he didn't get some rest. But he couldn't help it. The more he pictured Anne and Johnny together, the more unsettled he became.

Letting go of Anne Eicher was the last thing he wanted to do. Especially after he'd been dreaming of a happily ever after with her in his own home.

But now that he knew he wouldn't be moving in there with her, he'd lost his motivation for building. Who wanted to live in a brand-new farmhouse all alone? He needed someone to share it with. Someone to help him fill it with love and laughter and little ones. Someone to make the house into a home.

At this rate, he might as well put the property up for sale and move back in with his folks. But what if Charlotte and Glen bought it? Or, worse yet, Anne and Johnny. The unsettling thought twisted his gut. *Nee*, he wouldn't put it up for sale.

Gott, please show me what to do.

He rolled over and tried to make out the hands on the clock. Four o'clock. Might as well get up, make some coffee, and start the day. It was too bad he found no joy in it.

Nothing compared to last week when he could hardly keep his feet on the ground.

He'd contemplated writing his final secret admirer letter to Anne, but it had been her turn to write back. So, as soon as she did, he'd send one last letter telling her he wouldn't be writing anymore. He wasn't sure what exactly it would say, but he had a feeling the words would come when he needed them. They had thus far.

Andy glanced out the window as he fixed himself a simple breakfast. Sure enough, the clouds he'd seen last night had let loose overnight, creating a breathtaking wintry blanket of white outside.

He'd stop by *Mamm* and *Dat's* house before school and borrow their sleds. The scholars would be aching to slide down the hill behind the schoolhouse come recess time. And it would give them a reason to be extra *gut* during school.

He also needed to remind the scholars to tell their families about the blessing box. This time of year could be rough for those less fortunate in the community. A few families had already brought items, but the box wasn't half full yet. They only had two more weeks before the box would be delivered. If it wasn't filled up by then, Andy would take it upon himself to make a trip to the grocery store. Perhaps he should carve a few extra things—toys, maybe?—to add to the basket as well.

Just thinking about those less fortunate than himself made his own problems pale in comparison. Here he was lamenting not having a girlfriend when there were folks in the community who'd be celebrating Christmas this year without their loved ones.

Yet, his pain was real. No matter how hard he tried, he couldn't deny the chasm in his chest that had only grown since offering to give up Anne for Johnny.

He'd been contemplating what to say to her the next time he saw her. He honestly had no idea what he'd say. Last time he'd seen her, all he'd wanted to do was gather her in his arms and never let her go. But he couldn't do that now. Not when he knew Johnny was still in love with her and had in mind for them to marry.

Ach, why did love have to be so complicated? And why did it have to hurt so much when things went awry?

CHAPTER 15

An extra zap of energy had filled Anne while she fixed breakfast for the family and prepared their lunches. She had taken extra care with her appearance this morning, knowing that she'd likely be seeing Andy.

"You seem happy this morning," *Dat* remarked at breakfast.

"That's because she's dropping us off at school today and she'll be seeing Teacher Andy," Jane teased.

Anne gasped. Was her longing for Andy Stoltzfus evident to the whole world? Apparently so.

"Is that so, *dochder*?" *Dat* turned to her and sipped his coffee.

Anne dipped her head. "We're not courting or anything."

While she didn't really want to discuss this in front

of the *kinner*, it seemed inevitable.

"But they like each other. You should have seen how excited Teacher Andy got when Anne dropped off stuff for the blessing box. Smile as big as that crescent moon we had last night." Zane grinned.

Dat shrugged. "It's not a bad match. I like Andy Stoltzfus."

Hearing *Dat's* approval, along with Sammy's the night before, made her heart sing even louder.

"Do you think so?" She asked *Dat*. Her cheeks warmed as she glanced at her siblings, who seemed very intent on this particular conversation.

"I do." Then he sent a pointed look at Zane and Jane. "And this conversation does not leave this table. Do you understand?"

"*Jah, Dat*." The two youngest ones mumbled.

Although Anne wasn't sure *Dat's* admonition was enough to quell their excitement when they were with their friends at school. *Ach, vell*, it wasn't as though the gossip mill hadn't already started.

ANDY HAD a half hour to get himself together before the students began arriving. He was positively sure this would be one of the most grueling days of his life. He planned to stop by the Eichers' place and speak with

Anne today, although he was still unsure of what he'd say.

He glanced out the window, then held his breath as the Eichers' buggy pulled up beside the schoolhouse. Anne descended the buggy and tethered the horse to the hitching post but turned back as though speaking to Zane and Jane inside the buggy.

Then she ventured toward the schoolhouse alone, a bag in her hand.

As soon as the door opened, their gazes connected. *Ach*, how on earth was he going to say what he needed to say?

Her smile brightened as she made her way toward him, and his heart stuttered.

"I brought the outfits for the Christmas program. I hope they're okay." She reached into the bag. "And I also brought you more gingersnaps in case you ran out. I made up a fresh batch this morning."

He swallowed. "*Denki*, Anne." He took the plate from her hand and set it on the desk behind him.

"I'll be back to pick up the *kinner* after school. I didn't want them driving by themselves with the roads the way they are."

She turned to go, but he set a hand on her arm.

"Anne, wait."

Her eyebrows scrunched down. "*Jah*?"

Ach, she was so pretty. His insides were waging war

against him.

"I wanted to talk. About us." His heart needed to calm down before it raced right out of his chest.

Her expression widened as did her smile.

Nee, this wasn't going right.

"What I mean to say is that I really like you a lot." He frowned. Could she see the apology in his gaze? Did she know this was killing him? "As a *friend*. And I don't think that you and I are going to work..."

Her smile faltered and she held up her hand to stop his words. "I get it, Andy." She nodded vigorously, as tears formed in her eyes, then she hurried out of the schoolhouse like it had just caught fire.

"Anne, I'm sorry," he called after her just as the door slammed shut.

As soon as the *kinner* exited the buggy, Anne allowed her tears to fall. *Ach*, she felt like such a *dummkopp*!

She'd been so sure that Andy had shared her feelings. So sure that he was about to ask if he could court her.

How had she been so wrong? Had she been imagining things that weren't there?

Was he already involved in a relationship with

someone else?

Then she remembered the rumors about Teacher Andy courting someone. She *had* been imagining their mutual attraction. Or perhaps just hoping for it.

Ach, she'd made such a fool of herself showing up with cookies. What must he think of her? She must've seemed so desperate.

For sure and certain, she'd be sending Clive to fetch the *kinner* after school today. She couldn't bear to face Andy Stoltzfus again.

She shook the thought from her head.

Jah, she must've confused his intentions with her secret letter writer.

Ach, nee! She needed to snatch it out of the mailbox before the mailman arrived.

She thought of the words she'd penned.

Dear Secret Friend,

I'm sorry, but I feel like I have led you on by writing to you and that has not been my intention. The fact is, I've discovered someone here in my community that I am interested in. We're not courting yet, but I think our feelings are mutual.

So, with some regret, I need to tell

you that I won't be writing to you anymore. For what it's worth, know that I have enjoyed this experience and it will be something that I will always remember with fondness.

I hope you have a good life and that God will lead you to the one who is perfect for you.

Thank you for your friendship.

Sincerely,

Anne Eicher

ANDY HATED BEING the reason Anne's smile had dimmed. He'd hated lying to her about his feelings. He'd hated that he wouldn't get a chance to court her.

He'd ached to run after her and draw her into his arms and tell her that he hadn't meant it. That he was crazy about her. That he would marry her this instant if she'd let him.

But he couldn't do any of that. Soon, she'd see the truth of the matter—that Johnny loved her and she still loved him—and her heart would sing again.

As for himself, he wasn't sure he could ever find

that kind of bliss again.

Things would be a lot less complicated when Johnny came home.

Andy wouldn't have Anne for himself. But he'd feel a sense of satisfaction that Anne and Johnny were happy together. And knowing that he had a small part in Anne's happily ever after brought him some comfort. It would be bittersweet indeed.

Johnny said he'd be returning to the community and asking for Anne's hand in marriage as soon as the school semester was over. Andy was unsure why his cousin had even bothered with getting his high school equivalent diploma and college classes. It wasn't like he'd be using any of that extra education here in the community. His family were farmers and, as far as Andy knew, Johnny's classes had nothing to do with farming.

Unless...

The more he pondered the situation, the more he recalled Johnny's previous words about convincing Anne to leave the Amish with him. Had that been his intention all along? *Ach*, he needed to have another talk with his cousin to be sure and certain. Because the last thing he or anyone else in their community wanted was for Anne Eicher to be led away from their people.

Had he made a mistake in offering to give up Anne so readily?

CHAPTER 16

Anne pulled the buggy up to the mailbox, then frowned when she realized it was empty. Surely their mailman hadn't arrived this early, had he? *Ach*. She supposed it was possible since they did get busier over the holiday season.

There went her plan to snatch the letter out. How had she managed to lose both Andy and her secret admirer all in the same day? And it wasn't even nine o'clock yet!

Perhaps she should have stayed in bed.

"Anne?"

Her head whipped around toward the house. "Johnny? What are you doing here?"

He took the reins from her hands and led the horse to the hitching post. "Can we talk?"

She shrugged, then stepped down from the buggy. Surely this day couldn't get any worse, could it? "*Jah*. It's too cold out here, though. Let's go inside."

"I'll put up your horse, then come in."

She took in Johnny's Amish clothes. Had he come back to the community? What did this visit mean?

Anne headed inside. She sighed as she opened the tap from the back of the woodstove and poured hot water into two mugs. Johnny would want a hot cup of coffee. She'd offer him gingersnaps, but he'd never cared much for them.

She frowned as she thought of the first time she'd given gingersnaps to Andy. He'd been so excited. Surely she hadn't imagined his kiss to her hand. That had been more than just a thank you, hadn't it?

Something wasn't adding up, but she couldn't place her finger on it.

The mudroom door opened and closed with a gust of cool air. Johnny blew warmth into his hands and stepped further into the kitchen.

"Oh, *gut*. You made me coffee?"

She'd always found his puppy-dog eyes attractive. It was one of the things she'd been drawn to in the first place.

She handed him the mug and his fingers slipped around it.

He plunked himself down at the table. "It sure is getting cold out there, *ain't not*?"

She remained standing. "Why are you here, Johnny?"

"I was hoping to talk you into giving us another try." He lifted those irresistible eyes to hers.

"I already expressed my thoughts about that in the letter I sent you." Her hands planted on her hips.

"I know. But just hear me out, Anne." He pushed his coffee forward. "We could get married here as soon as the bishop would let us."

"What about your *Englisch* life? Aren't you going to school?" She tapped her foot.

"I'm coming up on a break." He stood and reached for her hands. "Anne, I know you'd love it in the *Englisch* world. There are so many things to see and do. You don't have to live by any Ordnung. You'll have freedom."

"*Jah*, but at what cost? I won't lose my family, Johnny. Not for you. And not for anyone else." She shook her head, surprised she'd listened to him thus far. "Besides, I'm needed here."

"What about Andy?"

Her gaze narrowed on his. "What about Andy?"

"I bet you're willing to leave your family for him."

"I don't know what you're talking about, Johnny."

"Oh, don't you? So, you two haven't been spending time together? Or has he been making all that up? And I know for a fact you've been writing him letters. I've seen them myself."

"I haven't been writing...wait. Are you saying that Andy is my secret admirer?" Her cheeks warmed. *Ach*, she'd been right.

He scratched his head. "Well, I..." He sighed. "Please don't tell Andy I spilled the beans. I told him I wouldn't say anything."

"Well, then, why did you? He obviously misplaced his trust when he put it you. Imagine that, another thing we have in common." She studied him. "Did you ask Andy to step aside because you were coming back?"

"Well, I...look, Anne—"

"Did you or not?"

"No, I mean, not really. When I told him that I still loved you and wanted to marry you, he said that he would end things with you. He voluntarily gave you up so we could be together." He reached for her hand again, but she pulled away.

"I'm not going to marry you, Johnny. I'm sorry. But when you left, it opened my eyes to a few things."

"What things?"

"Well, for one, we don't have the same goals in life.

Two, I'm staying in the community and you're not. Three, I've realized that I need someone more steady. Someone who wants to walk in the ways of *Gott*. Someone—"

"Like Andy." He nodded. "I get it, Anne.

"I don't want to hurt you, but I think that deep inside, I'm not really what *you're* looking for either. You need someone who shares your desires and passions. That isn't me."

"You're right. I guess I just got jealous when Andy started getting letters from you. And he would come back to the apartment and I would see how happy he was. I just knew it was because he was in love with you, and I'd lost you for good."

Anne's heart began an erratic cadence. "Wait. You think that Andy *loves* me?"

"Without a doubt. The only reason he stepped aside is because he thought you would be happier with me. After all, we'd courted for over five years."

"Andy loves me." Anne couldn't help the smile from spreading across her face.

"I can see now that you love him too. Why don't you go tell him?" Johnny smiled now.

"I already did. Kind of. I sent him a letter..."

Johnny pulled an envelope from his jacket. "You mean this?"

She snatched the envelope from his hand and

whacked him across the arm with it. "You stole my mail?"

"The flag was up, and I was curious. Besides, if you'd agreed to marry me, you might have changed your mind about sending it."

"You're right. I have."

CHAPTER 17

Today had been one of the worst days Andy had ever experienced. Second only to the day he'd found Charlotte and Glen kissing under the covered bridge.

He tried his best to look on the positive side, but all he could think about was spending the rest of his life all alone in what would soon be his brand-new house. And that thought stank.

He'd attempted to convince himself that he could find another woman to love, but when he thought of his remaining possibilities there was no one who sparked his interest. Not like the Eicher women had.

He sighed as he pulled his horse onto his property. Visions of Anne filled his mind each time he opened the trailer door. If he could go back to the last time she'd been there, he would kiss her on the lips instead of her hand. Because at least then he would know what it felt like to have her in his arms.

Perhaps he was just a glutton for punishment.

Nee. He shook the thought away. That would've been wrong. Especially in light of Johnny's plan to propose to her.

He took care of his horse, making sure the mare had food and water. When the weather turned cold, he had to break the ice so she'd have something to drink. He hadn't needed to do that yet, but with the upcoming forecast of snow and ice storms, there was a *gut* chance the water would be freezing soon.

As he neared the trailer, something white attached to the door caught his eye. Someone had been here.

He snatched the envelope and hastily opened it, curiosity getting the better of him. *Ach*, it was from Anne. He'd become quite familiar with her penmanship since they'd begun sending letters back and forth.

His lips twisted when he read the opening greeting.

Dear Secret Friend,

Wait. *Secret friend?* How did she know it was him? *Ach*, Johnny must've told her! He huffed, then gritted his teeth. Johnny had promised not to tell.

He shoved his frustration away and shook his head. What did it even matter now? It didn't. He'd lost her.

His eyes continued to scan the letter.

I don't know how to tell you this. My ex-boyfriend Johnny came back into my life and asked me to marry him.

Andy stopped reading. Did he really want to continue this torture? *Nee*, but he had to read all the words, no matter how much they hurt. He needed to face reality.

I told him no.

Wait. He read that last line again.

I told him no.

She said no? His heartbeat quickened. Then he continued.

I told him that I was no longer interested in a relationship with him. I told him that I had fallen in love with someone else.

And that someone else is you, Andy Stoltzfus.

What? He read that last line again.

And that someone else is you, Andy Stoltzfus.

Ach. This was...was this real?

Yes, I discovered you were my secret admirer. Johnny confirmed what I had already suspected. He also told me that you were in love with me. Is this true?

Yes, it's true! *So true.*

Because if it is, then my answer to the question in your first letter is yes.

Wait. *What*? What was she saying?
Ach, he had to go see her! If this meant what he

thought it meant...excitement surged throughout his entire being.

He turned around and rushed back toward the barn.

"Andy!" A beautiful voice called from behind.

He spun around, his heart stuttering all over the place. There, in the doorway of his trailer, stood the only Christmas gift he wanted this year. Anne Eicher.

"Where are you going?" She giggled, and the sound of her melodic voice all but brought him to tears.

Was this really happening?

"I was going to see you." He ran toward the trailer.

She stepped back as he dashed up the two steps, his breath heavy with excitement.

"What did you mean by that? What question did you say yes to?" His eyes searched hers and it took everything in him not to close the distance between them. But he needed to know first.

"That I would agree to marry you." A becoming blush blossomed, painting her features pink.

He closed the door behind him, and he was immediately enveloped in warmth. He was unsure if it was due to the trailer's propane heater or the presence of this beautiful woman standing before him.

He could no longer refrain.

His hands reached out and cradled her impossibly soft face. First, his fingertips explored her eyelids.

Then, her cheekbones. Next, they roamed her jawline. And finally, glided over her perfect lips.

This was a moment to be cherished. A moment to be remembered.

He could scarcely believe this was real.

"Anne Eicher, I love you." The whispered words left his lips right before he claimed hers.

She leaned into his kiss, but stepped back until she was up against the small refrigerator. Her form melded to his as their kiss became more intent with each breath they exchanged. When a soft moan escaped her lips, he deepened the kiss and drew her fully into his arms.

Several moments later, they broke apart, desperate for air.

Anne managed to find her voice. "But there's one condition, Andy Stoltzfus." She traced his jawline, not taking her eyes from his.

"What's that?" His lips tipped at the corners.

"I don't want to wait until next Christmas to marry you."

He swallowed. "You don't?"

"*Nee*. You see, I'm hoping that next Christmas it won't be *just us* celebrating." Her color darkened at the bold words.

"Won't just be..." His eyes widened. "You mean... Oh. *Oh*." What felt like was probably a really goofy grin filled his features. "I think we can try for that."

"*Gut*. I hope so."

"I'll talk to Bishop Omar tomorrow to see how soon we can get a date."

She studied him, her grin widening even more.

"What? What's that smile for?"

She lifted a shy shoulder shrug. "I may have already taken the liberty to talk to the bishop. How does the first Tuesday after Second Christmas sound?"

"It sounds like the best Christmas gift you could ever give me." His voice turned husky and his greedy mouth found hers once again.

ANDY WAS PLEASED that the school Christmas program had gone off without a hitch. Anne helped him deliver not one blessing box, but two to needy families in the community. The boxes had been overflowing with food, clothing, and gifts for each of the family members.

For the hurting families, it wasn't as *gut* as having their missing loved one there with them, but he was thankful his classroom could be a small part of the joy they experienced this season.

He already had an idea for the scholars' next goodwill project—asking each child to craft handmade cards and write a joke inside. He knew the cards would bring a smile when they delivered them to the shut-ins in their community.

He and Anne would be attending a youth event tonight—caroling in the community, then ice skating and snacks at the Lapp family's farm.

Upon hearing their engagement published in the *bans* on Sunday, some of the men in the community had come to him to volunteer their time to help build his house. He and Anne would need it soon. But he and Anne had become fond of his little camper. He suspected the memories made there would live in their hearts for years after the trailer was gone.

He recalled one of their recent memories.

He'd come home expecting an empty trailer. And it *had* been empty with the exception of greenery added to his ceiling. There appeared to be small bunches hanging all over the camper's interior.

"What on earth?" He chuckled.

He heard a giggle from behind the accordion door that led to his small bedroom, then suddenly it opened and Anne appeared.

He had a difficult time containing his smile. "What is this?" He pointed to the ceiling.

"Sammy said the *Englischers* have a tradition. They hang mistletoe in the doorways and on the ceilings and such." Her cheeks took on a beautiful pink hue. "And when two people love each other, they stand under the mistletoe and kiss."

His lips twitched. "Is that so?"

She shrugged, suddenly shy. "That's what they say."

He stepped closer. "Well, far be it from me to prove them wrong."

At that, he took her into his arms, making them both wish that they'd married a few days sooner.

EPILOGUE

T*he following Christmas...*

"Silent Night! Holy Night!" The melody floated from outside through the walls of the Stoltzfus home.

Andy bent down to where Anne sat in the bed and kissed her on the lips. "It sounds like we have Christmas carolers. I'd better not leave them out in the snow."

Anne watched as her husband rushed out of the room. She gazed down at the little one in her arms, too in love with their bundle of joy to do anything but smile. As a matter of fact, she was pretty sure the smile hadn't left hers or Andy's face since their little one made her appearance last night. Anne had gone to sleep smiling and had woken up with a smile.

Commotion lifted her gaze to the door of the bedroom. Just beyond the entrance stood *Dat*, Sammy, Charlotte, Clive, Jane, and Zane.

"Can we see the *boppli*?" Jane's smile blossomed.

"*Jah*. Of course. *Kumm* see her." She gestured them inside the room.

"What is her name?" Charlotte cooed to the little one. "Oh, she's so precious."

"We named her Sylvia. After *Mamm*." Anne's eyes lifted to *Dat*, and she didn't miss the dampness in his gaze. Then she glanced at each of her siblings. Each one's eyes also misted with tears.

"*Denki, dochder*. Your *mamm* would be delighted." *Dat* squeezed her hand.

"Would you like to hold her?" She held little Sylvia out to *Dat*. "You'd be the first one after me, Andy, and the midwife."

"I'd be honored to." *Dat* received the tiny bundle of joy into his arms, his eyes never leaving the *boppli*. "Perfect in every way. Just as *Der Herr* planned."

"I brought something for her." Charlotte beamed, holding out a present. "She'll appreciate it when she's a little older. But open it now."

Anne received the gift and smiled up at her beloved. She could hardly believe that the joy she now experienced existed in real life. She opened the carefully wrapped box and lifted out a book and a set of Raggedy Ann and Andy dolls. "*Ach*, like the ones we saw at the mall!"

"I knew I had to get them for you as soon as I heard Andy had proposed." Charlotte briefly glanced at Andy, then back to Anne.

"It's perfect, *schweschder. Denki*." Anne hugged Charlotte, remembering the time they'd gone to the mall to investigate who her secret admirer might be.

"Sounds like a story that needs to be told." Andy remarked, eyeing the two sisters.

"Someday." Anne promised, winking at Charlotte.

Anne's eyes met Andy's and all the love, joy, and peace of the Christmas season reflected in his gaze. *Gott* had truly blessed them.

And with the snowflakes outside dancing to the ground and their family gathered around, Anne never dreamed such joy could be found.

But it had.

Not in her husband. Not in her family. Not in her brand-new *boppli*.

But in Jesus, the Holy One of Israel, born over two thousand years ago in a lowly manger in Bethlehem. The Saviour of the world, residing in her heart today. A true joy. A lasting peace. A reason to celebrate all year round.

THE END

(Keep reading for a preview of my next book!)

ORDER DIRECT

Did you know you can order the **paperback** from your favorite retailer or **order directly** from me? Simply go to my website store at www.jenniferspredemann.com.

You can also request a physical mail order form at: jebspredemann@gmail.com

Or by writing to:

Jennifer Spredemann
PO BOX 70
CROSS PLAINS IN 47017

It's not too late to subscribe to my newsletter! Get a

FREE Amish story as my thank you gift when you sign up for my newsletter here: www.jenniferspredemann.com

LETTER FROM THE AUTHOR

Dear Reader,

Did you enjoy ***A Christmas Amish Courtship***?

I had fun writing this sweet love story between Anne and Andy, and I hope you've loved reading it!

I'd love to hear what your favorite scenes were. Do you have a favorite character? A favorite quote?

When I get to the end of a book, I tend to ponder the spiritual aspects. I particularly loved these words Andy penned to Anne: *I like to take something ordinary or broken and turn it into something beautiful. Kind of like what God does when we allow Him to work in our lives.*

Is your life broken or just ordinary? Are you simply going through the motions? If so, I'd like to challenge you to give your cares to God and allow Him to do His work in your life. I think we miss a lot because, as James said in the Bible, "Ye have not because ye ask not."

How many blessings are missing from our lives because we have simply failed to ask God? To include Him? That's probably an answer we'll never have this side of eternity.

Will you ask God for His guidance in your life? He may just turn what's broken into something beautiful.

Thanks for reading, friends!

To GOD be the glory!

Blessings in Christ,

Jennifer Spredemann

Heart-Touching Amish Fiction

P.S. Word of mouth is one of the best forms of advertisement and a HUGE blessing to the author. If you enjoyed this book, **please** consider leaving a review, sharing on social media, and telling your reading friends.

A SPECIAL THANK YOU

I want to say a special thank you to **Anita Whatley for suggesting Rose for Andy's mother and Ernestine Haggard for suggesting Sylvia for Anne's mother**. And thank you to all my readers who made suggestions! I love hearing from you.

I'd like to take this time to thank everyone that had any involvement in this book and its production, including my **mom** and **dad**, who have always been supportive of my writing, my longsuffering **family**—especially my handsome, encouraging **hubby**, my Amish and former-Amish **friends** who have helped immensely in my understanding of the Amish ways, my supportive **pastors** and **church** family, my **proofreaders**, my **editor**, my **formatters**, my **author friends**, my wonderful **readers** who buy, read, offer great input, and leave encouraging reviews and emails, my awesome **launch team** who, I'm confident, will 'Sprede the Word' about *A Christmas Amish Courtship!* And last, but certainly not least, I'd like to thank my ***Precious LORD and SAVIOUR JESUS CHRIST***, for without Him, none of this would have been possible!

If you haven't joined my Facebook reader group, you may do so here:
https://www.facebook.com/groups/379193966104149/

UNLIKELY SACRIFICE

(UNLIKELY AMISH CHRISTMAS) BOOK 5

JENNIFER SPREDEMANN

How much would you sacrifice for true love?

Brighton Parker is in his last year of school and his prospects for college are unbelievable. But he can't get the pretty Amish girl he met last summer at *Dawdi* Christopher's out of his head. The more time he spends with Bethany Byler, the more he realizes she's the one he wants to spend the rest of his life with.

Sure, his great grandparents are Amish, but none of his family is, and he has no Amish upbringing. But he knows that to be with Bethany in the forever sort of way, he'll have to alter his life drastically. Not to mention, he's quite certain his entire family will be against the notion—namely, his younger brother Jaycee who thinks he holds the world in his hands.

For Bethany to leave the Amish would be an even greater sacrifice for her. She'd lose her entire family, all her friends, and the tight-knit community she'd grown up in.

Another heart-touching story in the Unlikely Amish Christmas series!

Made in United States
Troutdale, OR
10/18/2024